MY LiFe
as a
Broken Bungee Cord

BOOKS BY BILL MYERS

Teen Books
Hot Topics, Tough Questions
Christ B.C.

Children's Series
McGee and Me! (12 books)

The Incredible Worlds of Wally McDoogle
—*My Life As a Smashed Burrito with Extra Hot Sauce*
—*My Life As Alien Monster Bait*
—*My Life As a Broken Bungee Cord*
—*My Life As Crocodile Junk Food*

Fantasy Series
Journeys to Fayrah:
—*The Portal*
—*The Experiment*
—*The Whirlwind*
—*The Tablet*

the incredible worlds of **Wally McDoogle**

MY LiFe as a Broken Bungee Cord

BILL MYERS

WORD PUBLISHING
Dallas • London • Vancouver • Melbourne

MY LIFE AS A BROKEN BUNGEE CORD

Unless otherwise indicated, Scripture quotations are from the *International Children's Bible, New Century Version*, copyright © 1983, 1986, 1988 by Word Publishing.

Scripture quotations marked (NIV) are from The New International Version of the Bible, copyright © 1978 by the New York International Bible Society.

Instructions for making a model balloon (pages 27-30) are based on information in *Ballooning: The Complete Guide to Riding the Winds* by Dick Wirth and Jerry Young. Copyright © 1991 Marshall Editions Developments, Ltd. Copyright © 1980 by Marshall Editions, Ltd.

Library of Congress Cataloging-in-Publication Data

Myers, Bill, 1953–
    My life as a broken bungee cord / Bill Myers.
        p. cm. — (The Incredible worlds of Wally McDoogle ; #3.)
"Word kids!"
    Summary: When he takes part in a hot-air balloon race, twelve-year-old Wally, computer whiz and "human catastrophe," learns what it means to fully put his trust in God.
    ISBN 0–8499–3404–4
    [1. Hot-air balloons—Fiction. 2. Balloon ascensions—Fiction. 3. Christian life—Fiction. 4. Humorous stories.] I. Title. II. Series: Myers, Bill, 1953– Incredible worlds of Wally McDoogle ; #3.
PZ7.M98234Mye   1993
[Fic]—dc20   92–45182
                                                 CIP
                                               AC

Printed in the United States of America

3 4 5 6 7 8 9 LBM 9 8 7 6 5 4 3 2 1

Thanks to *Balloon Adventures*—
For a great ride and a great adventure.

" . . . trust God all the time. Tell him all your problems. God is our protection."

—Psalm 62:8

Contents

Chapter 1

Just for Starters . . .

AUGHHHHHHHHHHHHH!

That's what you're supposed to say when you're falling toward the earth at a zillion miles an hour. And, always being careful to obey the rules, I gave it everything I had. . . .

AUGHHHHHHHHHHHHHHHH!

I wasn't sure where I was. I wasn't sure how I got there. But I had a pretty good idea where I was going. Something about the way the trees, houses, and ground all raced at me gave the distinct impression I was about to make a *distinct impression*. The ground and I would soon become inseparable buddies.

Then I heard it. . . .

"Hey, McDoogle—hey, Dork-oid!"

I looked around. There was nobody in sight. Well, unless you count the bald eagle that was in a nose dive directly beside me.

"You talking to me?" I shouted over the roaring wind.

"You see any other Dork-oids?" he called.

I glanced around. He had a point.

"So," he continued, "you all ready for spring vacation?"

I looked to the ground. It was three hundred feet away. "It doesn't look like I'll be around for spring break this year."

"Why not?" he asked.

"I'm allergic to dying. I break out into a bad case of death every time it happens."

The bird cackled. "That's good, McDoogle—you ought to write that in your next story."

"Yeah," I said, glancing back to the rushing ground, "but I'm not that fast of a typist."

"Too bad."

"Listen, I don't want to be nosy, but exactly where am I—how did I get here?"

"Get where?" the bird asked, as he began to preen his tail feathers.

"Here . . . you know, ready to die."

"Oh, this. Haven't you figured it out?"

"Figured what out?"

"It's a dream," the bird called.

"What is?"

"This is. How else could I be talking?"

"Oh, yeah, of course, a dream." Suddenly I felt more relaxed. I glanced back to the ground. It was still coming at us pretty fast. "Uh, listen. It's been awhile since I've had one of these things. . . . I forget, when you hit the ground in a dream, do you feel pain?"

"Nah."

"Good."

"If you hit the ground in a dream you die."

Not so good. Suddenly I didn't feel so relaxed. Suddenly I felt your usual raw, white-knuckled, panic-stricken terror!

BEEP BEEP BEEP BEEP . . .

"What's that beeping?" I shouted.

"My telephone pager."

"Telephone pager?"

The bird shrugged. "Hey, it's your dream, McDoogle, not mine."

"Yeah, but—"

"Listen, I better be going. Have a nice day."

"YOU JUST CAN'T LEAVE ME HERE! WHAT AM I SUPPOSED TO DO?"

"Got me. Though I kinda liked that screaming stuff you were doing." With that he gave two mighty thrusts of his wings and was gone.

I looked back to the ground. I knew I was in trouble when I could count the blades of grass in the approaching lawn, so I did what I did best . . .

"AUGHHHHHHHHHHHH!"

"Hey, Wally. Wally, wake up."

I felt a finger jabbing into my ribs. I wished it would jab a little harder 'cause right now I could see the bugs crawling between those blades of grass. . . .

"Wally, you gotta see this. Wally, wake up."

My eyes fluttered open. *"Mumph umph mazrabballa,"* I said. It was supposed to be, "Thanks for saving my life," but for the moment that was the best I could come up with.

"Wally, look out the window!" The voice belonged to Wall Street, my best friend, a Latino girl. Not only did the voice belong to her, but so did the finger digging into my ribs.

"Ow! Rumphel mul somnada!" (Translation: "Knock it off with the open heart surgery, will ya!")

"He's over on this side now." A new voice said. It belonged to Wall Street's mom.

Suddenly reality flooded in. We were riding in Wall Street's mom's station wagon—me, Wall Street, and Opera, my other best friend. It was spring break. Her mom had talked our folks into letting us ride with them to the mountains and visit Wall Street's brother.

KWOOOOOOOOSHHHHHH!

"What's that?" I muttered, grateful that my mouth was finally working in English.

"It's Miguel!" Wall Street cried. She quickly rolled down the window and stuck out her head.

Opera was up in the front seat doing the same.

So was Wall Street's mom.

But not me. No sir. I was an individual. Just because everybody else did it was no reason for me to do it. I was no follower; I was a leader.

KWOOOOOOOOOOSHHHHH!

Then again, even leaders need a little fresh air.

I rolled down my window and stuck my head into the cold mountain air. I couldn't believe it. Directly over our car was a gigantic hot-air balloon. A guy was standing in the basket below it waving and shouting.

"Hello down there!"

"Mickey, is that you?" Wall Street cried from the other side of the car.

"Hey, Sis!" The guy reached up and squeezed a lever. Suddenly:

KWOOOOOOOOOOSHHHH! . . . a giant flame leaped out of a burner thingie above his head. It shot half a dozen feet into the balloon, making it rise a little bit. When he turned it off, he shouted back down to us.

"Tell Momma to take that left turn coming up and follow me! There's a pasture a quarter mile ahead. I'll touch down there. My friend Kenny's already there with the chase car."

He squeezed the lever, and it let out with another . . .

KWOOOOOOOOOOOOSHHH! . . . before he disappeared over the tree tops.

"That fool!" Wall Street's mom cried before rattling off a bunch of Spanish. Wall Street's mom always rattled off Spanish when she got upset.

"I didn't know your brother flew hot-air balloons," Opera shouted over the Walkman that was permanently attached to his ears.

Wall Street grinned. "Miguel's always trying weird stuff."

It was good to see her grin about her brother. Usually, whenever his name came up, she'd get all quiet or just shrug. I guess there was a big showdown between her mom and brother awhile back. He'd quit college, then run off to work at some mountain resort. Wall Street said his letters sounded like he didn't even believe in God anymore.

She was pretty upset about the whole thing. First her dad left them, and now her brother. I can't tell you how many times she brought up Miguel's name in Sunday school. It seemed to be all she ever prayed about.

Suddenly Wall Street's mom turned the car to the left. We skidded off the pavement and onto a gravel road. (Besides speaking Spanish when she's upset, she also drives a little crazy.) We pulled ourselves up off the floor and crawled back into our seats.

"There he is!" Opera pointed. "Dead ahead!"

It was like a dream, the way the giant balloon hovered in front of us, slowly dropping lower and lower. All the time Miguel stood in the basket carefully looking down, and occasionally firing the burner thingie.

We rounded a bend. Suddenly we were at the field. Wall Street's mom hit the brakes. We hit the floor.

She threw open the door and raced across the field after the balloon. "Mickey, Mickey, Mickey!"

We crawled back up, shoved open our doors, and followed.

Miguel's friend Kenny was also running toward the balloon. Not far away stood a rusty, old pickup with a giant X painted on top.

After Momma came Wall Street. Then Opera. And finally, yours truly. I would have been in the lead, but stepping on untied shoe laces and falling flat on your face tends to slow you down a little.

"Watch out for this barbed wire!" Wall Street shouted back to us.

"Got it," Opera yelled as he side-stepped it.

"What barbed wire?" I shouted. "I don't see any—"

TRIP . . . TUMBLE TUMBLE POKE POKE.

"OW!"

I found it. Actually it found me. Suddenly my pants and the wire were one.

Meanwhile the balloon dropped lower and lower until finally the basket skimmed the bushes. A couple of nearby cows looked up a moment before returning to their afternoon grass snack.

At last the basket touched down and started dragging across the ground.

"Mickey, Mickey, Mickey!" his mom kept shouting as she raced toward him.

Miguel pulled a rope that opened the top of the balloon, and suddenly the entire thing began to collapse. Kenny was the first to arrive. He grabbed hold of the basket to keep it steady. Next came Miguel's mom.

"Mickey, Mickey, Mickey!"

He scrambled out of the basket and threw out his arms (either to protect himself or to hug her, it was hard to tell which).

"Mickey, Mickey, *OOAAAFFFF!*" she grunted as they hit.

"*OOAAAFFFF!*" he grunted as he staggered under the blow.

A second later Wall Street joined them. Then Opera. The balloon was still inflated and flapping in the breeze.

"Sis!" Miguel shouted. "You and your friend grab the canopy. Help Kenny, here, get out all the hot air."

Wall Street and Opera hopped to it like pros.

I would have hopped to it like a pro, but I was still hung up like a goon. I'd had a couple of minutes to get untangled from the wire, which, of course, meant I was more tangled than ever. Besides my pants, I'd now snagged my red sweatshirt . . . my socks . . . my shoes . . . my belt . . . even my wristwatch.

The cows glanced over to me with boredom. I guess they'd already heard of my reputation for gracefulness, so they just went back to munching.

"Well, at least there aren't any bulls," I muttered to myself. "With this red sweatshirt, things could really get out of hand if there was a—"

Moooo!

I froze. Somehow that moo sounded a little too macho to be a cow.

MooooOOOO!

It also sounded a little too mean. I looked over my shoulder.

MOOOOOOOOOOOOO!!!

Uh-oh.

Chapter 2

Bully for Me

"RUN, WALLY! RUN!"

I'd already figured that part out. When a giant bull charges at you full speed, you decide that stuff pretty early. I sprinted across the field as fast as I could. Unfortunately, "as fast as I could" was a little slower than "as fast as the bull could."

He gained on me with every step!

Of course, it would have helped if I had had my shoes on . . . or my socks . . . or any other stitch of clothing. But I'd left them all hanging back on the barbed-wire fence.

Now it was just me and my Fruit of the Looms!

"GO, WALLY! GO!"

I was going, I was going! But so was Bully Boy. I could hear him breathing and snorting right behind me!

"Jump over the fence!" Miguel called. "Jump over the fence!"

They stood up ahead on the other side of a wooden fence, cheering me on.

I threw a look over my shoulder . . . a bad idea. Sometimes if you're going to die, it's best not to know the details—like how sharp the hoofs are, how far the horns stick out, how angry the eyes bulge.

By the looks of things this guy was definitely in the mood for a little snack. A human shish kabob to be exact. He obviously wanted me to "stick around" for dinner. Now, I like eating out as much as the next guy. I'm just not crazy about being the main course!

"GO, WALLY, GO!"

The fence was just feet from me. Unfortunately, the bull was *just inches!*

"JUMP, WALLY! JUMP! JUMP!"

It was now or never. I leaped into the air and gave it everything I had. Everyone watched in awe as I sailed high and far. It was a gorgeous leap. Everything was perfect. Well, except for the part where I hit the fence. . . .

"OAAFFF!"

. . . on the wrong side.

Well, that about wrapped it up for living. In a second Bully Boy and I would begin a game of darts—with me being the dart board!

Too bad. There were so many things I had
wanted to do before I died . . . like quarterback the
Dallas Cowboys, travel to Mars, shave.
But none of that would happen. It was all over—
except the funeral, which I probably wouldn't
hang around for anyway. They're always so de-
pressing . . . especially when they're your own.
Suddenly Miguel's big hands grabbed me by the
shoulders and dragged me over the top board of
the fence. That was the good news. The bad news
was he managed to scrape off a few layers of my
skin in the process. . . .
"OW! OW! OOO, THAT SMARTS!"
But a few chunks of skin was a small price to
pay for the rest of my flesh. Suddenly:
CRASH!
The bull hit the fence. Everybody screamed.
Well, everybody but me. Being the courageous
type that I am, I didn't let out a peep. No sir, not
a shout, not even a whimper. It's hard to scream
when you've already passed out.

＊　＊　＊　＊　＊

"So . . . OW! . . . how long . . . OUCH! . . . have
you been . . . OOO! . . . working for this resort?" I
sat next to a big stone fireplace in the hotel lobby

talking to Miguel. I was also pulling out thorns from my tender tootsies. Thanks to Miguel's quick thinking, the bull didn't get me. Thanks to leaving my shoes and socks on the fence, the thorns and thistles did.

"I've been working here about four months," he said.

"It's really beautiful up here." Wall Street sighed as she gazed out the picture window at all the mountains and trees. "You think we'll get the chance to go camping?"

"No way!" Opera shouted over his Walkman. The guy always shouted over his Walkman. But he didn't listen to heavy metal. No sir, Opera didn't get his name for his love of "Guns 'n Roses." It was Mozart to the max. Haydn to the hilt. Rock and rollin' with Rossini. In short, the guy loved classical music . . . almost as much as he hated the great outdoors.

"Come on, Opera," I teased. "You should get out there and experience the elements."

Opera scowled. "If God wanted us to experience the elements, He wouldn't have invented central heating and air-conditioning."

"What are you afraid of?" I persisted.

"Nothing, unless you count the little things like avalanches, flash floods, tornadoes, hurricanes, forest fires . . . then, of course, there are those lovely bears, cougars, wolves, skunks, bats, coyotes, ticks, rattlesnakes, scorpions, mosquitoes—"

"Mosquitoes?"

"Hey, I worked hard for my blood. Why should I share it?"

"But Opera," Miguel interrupted, "once you understand the wilderness and learn to respect it, there isn't that much to fear."

"Unless you're flying balloons or doing other foolhardy things," his mom argued.

"Momma," he turned toward her. "I'm twenty years old. That's my job. As recreational director, one of the things I do is take guests up in the balloon."

"Madness." She shook her head. "Utter madness."

"Momma, I've studied and taken tests. I'm fully qualified to—"

"You could have done that at home. They have balloons at home. Why quit school? Why move halfway across the state, away from your only family?" Suddenly her voice began to quiver and sound a little high.

"Momma," Miguel spoke soothingly as he crossed the room to where she was sitting. "Momma . . . we've got four days together . . . please, let's don't spend it arguing. Okay?" He reached out and touched her arm. "Okay?"

She bit her lip and nodded. It was pretty obvious she was fighting back tears. I threw a look over to Wall Street. She was doing her own version of lip chewing. You could tell she really loved the guy.

Finally Opera cleared his throat. "So if we're like guests here, does that mean we can go up in the balloon, too?"

"Sure," Miguel answered. "We could do it tomorrow if you want."

Wall Street's face brightened.

Her mom's darkened.

And mine? Well, mine started sweating. Like a fire hose. You see, heights and me, we're not the best of friends. In fact, remember that little dream I had about falling with the eagle? Technically, that wasn't a dream—it was a nightmare. Like the type I've had at least once a month for as long as I can remember.

Mom says it came from some childhood trauma. Dad says it's something I'll grow out of when I become a real man. Burt and Brock, my twin brothers, say it's 'cause the doctor dropped me on my head.

The point is I'm so scared of heights that I get dizzy just stepping up on street curbs. No way was I riding in some overgrown kid's toy!

* * * * *

An hour later Opera and I were up in our room unpacking. Well, Opera was unpacking. I was pulling out ol' Betsy, my laptop computer. This sudden exposure to fresh air and nature had already started me thinking of another story. . . .

"Go long, go long!" Ecology-Man shouts as he runs from a charging moose and fires off a perfect pass. The crowd of forest animals cheers as the football (actually, a 3 1/2 pound rainbow trout) spins through the air. (Don't worry, rainbow trout love to spin.)

At the far end of the field a grizzly bear stretches his paws high into the air. But the trout is too high above ol' Griz's head to catch. The overgrown fur ball must leap into the air. Looking like Michael Jordan in a fur coat, the bear makes a tremendous jump. He catches the slippery seafood and races toward the goal line.

The forest creatures cheer.

Griz is at the 15-yard line, the 10,
the 5 . . . and then, just when everyone is sure he's going to score, that
they'll win and go on to the "Super
Brawl," Griz pops the delicious tidbit
into his mouth and swallows it whole.

The crowd groans. Wolves howl, crows
cry, and slugs . . . uh . . . slime.

"No, no, no," Ecology-Man shouts.
"You're supposed to run with the ball,
not eat it!"

Ol' Griz shrugs with a sheepish smile
and a rather loud burp.

Ecology-Man shakes his head. For years
he's tried to teach his forest friends
the fine art of football, and for years
he has failed.

Abandoned in the forest as a child,
Ecology-Man was raised by a family of
porcupines. Not a bad life, though it
made hugging and kissing a little . . .
(here it comes) . . . sticky . . . (hey,
I warned you). He didn't remember much
of his human past — except how his older
brothers, Burt and Brock, always hogged
the TV for Monday night football.

As he grew, he learned to call upon
the powerful forces of nature, like

wind, rain, fire, and underarm odor. He
also became best buds with all the
forest creatures. (Well, except for
those slug guys . . . and you really
can't blame him for that. Ever try to
slap a slug on the back over a good
laugh? It can get a little messy, unless
you're wearing a raincoat and safety
goggles.)

Suddenly, a swarm of bees swoop down
onto the field. They race to our *bio-*
degradable[1] big boy bearing the bulging
biceps and buzz his beanie. (Say that
five times fast.) He strains to make out
what they're saying, but they're too
excited.

He shouts back, "Bzz . . . Bzzzbzz .
. . Bz . . . Bzzzzzzzzz! Bzzzzzz . . .
Bz . . . Bz . . . Bzzzz . . . Bzzzzz
bzzzzzz! Bzzzzzz . . . bzzzzz . . . "

(Translation: *"Say what?"*)

Instead of going through all that again
(thank goodness), the bees drop to the
grass and spell out their message . . .

"T O X O I D   B R E A T H !"

---

1. BIODEGRADABLE: easily broken down and
decomposed by nature.

Ecology-Man gasps. The mechanical monster Toxoid Breath is on the loose! Created by the mad industrial scientist Marcus Make-a-Buck, this giant robot storms through the environment, killing everything in its path.

His methods are endless, but the results are always the same . . .

Bye-bye birdies, hello freeways and shopping malls.

Suddenly there is a loud crash, the splintering of trees, and the roar of an old-fashioned, eight-cylinder, gas guzzler.

Ecology-Man spins around as the robot smashes out of the forest and rolls toward him on its giant tank-tread feet. It is no taller than a man, but stretches as wide as an eight-lane freeway.

"TOXOID BREATH!" our hero cries.

The mechanical monster laughs. Chemical waste drools from the corners of its lips. Suddenly it exhales a cloud of poisonous gas at our *environmentally-safe*[2] hero. But that's okay, Ecology-Man visited Los Angeles; he knows all about breathing poisonous air.

---

2. ENVIRONMENTALLY SAFE: not harmful to the environment.

Next, Toxoid Breath reaches down and snaps on the stereo in its iron belly. Suddenly the peace of the forest is destroyed by the blasting noise of the heavy metal group . . . "MegaEverything." The noise pollution blows over trees, forces animals to race for cover . . . and, worst of all, musses our hero's hair!

That's right. Ecology-Man's hair is no longer perfectly plastered in place! Now he's mad . . . real mad. He thrusts out his manly jaw and calls to the forces of nature—

"Hey, Wally, you gonna turn that light off or what?"

I looked up. Opera was already in bed. I glanced at my watch. It was nearly 10:00.

"Sorry," I said as I pressed F10 and shut ol' Betsy down for the night. "I was really getting into that story."

"No sweat," Opera said. "But we're going to need our sleep, if we're going up in the balloon early tomorrow morning."

The word hit me like a ton of bricks. Not the word *sleep*, not the word *early*, not even the word *balloon*. It was that other word . . . the "u" word.

The one that starts with "u" and ends in "p" and doesn't have any letters in between.

"Shouldn't . . ." my voice kinda cracked. "Shouldn't we, like, call up our folks and get permission first?" I asked.

"Already did." Opera yawned. "Miguel talked to both your parents and mine while you were up here typing."

"Oh," I said, already fearing the worst. "And?"

"And it's a 'GO'. . . first thing in the morning."

I tell you there are times you think your folks love you and times you're not so sure. But as I crawled under the sheets that night I no longer had a doubt. I could finally rest assured that they absolutely, positively, in every way, shape, and form . . . HATED ME!

It looked like I was going up in the balloon, which meant I was going to die. And as we all know, dying can really ruin your spring vacation.

Chapter 3

Up, Up and Away

At precisely 6:24 the following morning, I had it. I finally had proof that God really exists! And more importantly, I knew that He loved me . . . me, Wally Walking Disaster McDoogle.

Opera, Wall Street, and I were downstairs in the restaurant trying to eat (or drink) the slimy, half-cooked eggs. Eating them wasn't the problem. Trying to get the slippery little fellows up to our mouths was the trick. Just when we were ready to trade in our forks for some straws, Miguel strolled in. "Bad news," he said. "It's too windy to go ballooning."

My soul sang, my spirit soared, my heart leaped.

"So," he said, "I guess we'll just have to wait until tomorrow."

My soul groaned, my spirit crashed, my heart fell on its face. I was still going to die. It was just going to be a day later. Either way it looked like there was going to be a definite lack of birthday gifts (let alone birthdays) in my future.

"So what do we do today?" Wall Street asked.

"Not camping!" Opera blurted out. "Or nature walks, or any of that outdoors junk!"

"Relax, Opera," Miguel said, breaking into an easy grin. "I've got something even you'll enjoy!"

"It doesn't involve hiking boots, sleeping bags, or freeze-dried anything, does it?"

Miguel chuckled. "Meet me down in the parking lot in two hours." He headed back toward the door. "Oh, and Sis?" He turned to Wall Street, "be sure to bring your hair dryer."

"My hair dryer? Why?"

"Two hours," he repeated. With that he turned and left.

The three of us looked at each other. *A hair dryer?*

Opera shrugged. Hair dryers meant electricity, which meant civilization, which meant he wasn't worried. So he caught the waitress's attention and did what he did best. "Excuse me, ma'am. Could I have some more of those delicious eggs . . . in a glass?"

*   *   *   *   *

A half hour later, Wall Street threw open Opera's and my door and stormed into our room.

"I hate him!" she cried. "I hate them both!"

I glanced down to Opera. He was on his knees with a half-eaten Twinkie trying to lure a cockroach out from under our dresser. I guess he was getting kind of bored with my company.

"Hate who?" I asked Wall Street as she plopped down on my bed.

She gave a good sniff and angrily wiped away the tears in her eyes. "God!... My brother!... My mother!... Everybody!"

Well, that about covered everyone I knew.

She continued. "Pastor Bergman's always saying if you pray for something hard enough and believe... and if it's the right thing, God will answer it."

"Yeah."

"Well, I've been praying ever since Mickey left home. I've been praying and believing that he'd come back again."

"And..."

"He's in the room going at it with Momma again. They're shouting and everything. No way is he coming back! All those prayers were a waste!"

"Wall Street," I tried to explain, "just 'cause you prayed—"

"I believed and everything, and it still didn't work!"

"Sometimes praying and having faith isn't—"

"If God can't answer a simple prayer like bringing my brother home, then maybe He can't answer any prayer!"

Before I could say anything, Wall Street hopped off the bed and stormed out of the room. She was pretty torn up. And she had a pretty good reason. Like I said, we prayed for her brother all the time in Sunday school—that he'd come home and start believing in God and everything. And now, after all that prayer, it sounded like things were worse than ever.

I really wanted to help, and I was sorry she'd left. But a part of me was also glad she'd gone. 'Cause that part of me had no idea what answer to give her.

*   *   *   *   *

Wall Street's hair dryer made it down to the parking lot, but she never did.

"Probably got some hot tips on the stock market," I joked. Wall Street was the only kid I knew who planned to make a million by the time she was fourteen.

Miguel nodded as he unwound the extension cord and plugged in the hair dryer. He knew the real reason she was gone. Like me, he knew it had nothing to do with making money or the stock market. He knew it was because of him.

Opera was beside us, finishing off his third bag of corn chips. He'd passed a vending machine in the lobby and thought he'd stock up till lunch. One thing you can say about Opera, he does love his empty calories. Don't get me wrong, the guy still believes in your four basic food groups. Only his four food groups are . . .

COOKIES, CHIPS, CHOCOLATE, AND CANDY.

"The four K's" he calls them. (Opera isn't so hot at spelling either.)

"So what's the plan?" I asked.

"Since it's too windy to use a real balloon, I figured we'd make a model one."

"Make?" I asked, nervously shoving my glasses back on my nose. "You mean, like, with our own hands?" Obviously this guy didn't fully appreciate my reputation for clumsiness. It's not that I'm a klutz, but how many people do you know throw their backs out when opening a pop can? Or electrocute themselves by turning on a light switch? Or whose parents call 911 whenever they see him carrying a hammer or screwdriver?

"That's right, you're going to make a model all by yourself."

"Maybe you should give the paramedics a call and have them stand by just in case," I offered.

Miguel reached into a bag and took out a bunch of foot-long squares of tissue paper—twenty-seven to be exact. Also some glue, scissors, paper clips, and wire (all instruments of death in my inexperienced hands). Then he told us what to do.

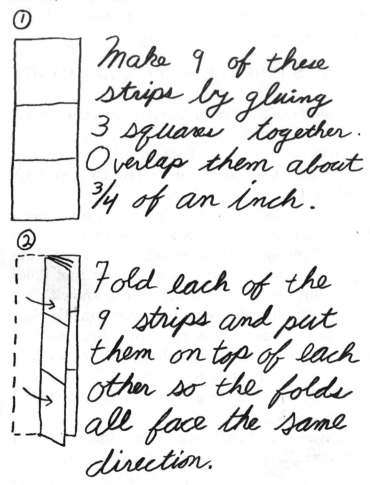

① Make 9 of these strips by gluing 3 squares together. Overlap them about ¾ of an inch.

② Fold each of the 9 strips and put them on top of each other so the folds all face the same direction.

③

Paper clip the strips together and draw half of a spear head on the top strip. Cut along that outline.

④

Glue the curved edges of these strips to each other (overlap ½"). When they're dry fold the glued seams back on themselves and glue again.

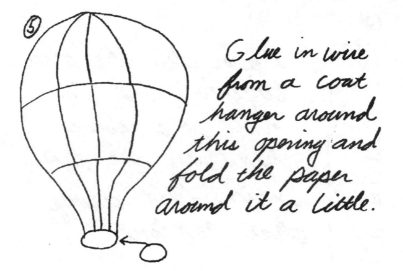

⑤ Glue in wire from a coat hanger around this opening and fold the paper around it a little.

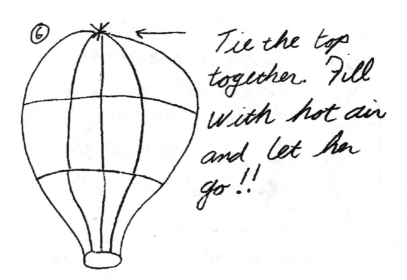

⑥ Tie the top together. Fill with hot air and, let her go!!

Before I knew it, Opera and I were working up a storm. (I've thrown in some diagrams and instructions in case you're interested in making your own.)

There were a few minor setbacks, like the glue bottle that was all plugged up till I squished and squeezed and . . .

KEEEERSPLATTT!

. . . it exploded on everyone.

Then there were the scissors. Somehow my T-shirt and jeans wound up more cut than the paper. And someday I'll have to apologize to Opera for the big chunks of hair missing from the back of his head (if he ever finds out).

In a couple of hours we were all finished. We had ourselves a giant, three-foot-tall, paper balloon.

"I still don't know why we need the hair dryer," Opera said.

"Watch and be amazed." Miguel smiled as he shoved the hair dryer inside the balloon and snapped it on.

Our balloon immediately began to fill with air. And as it filled, it started to rise.

"Grab hold of it; don't let it get away," Miguel ordered.

"Why's it rising like this?" Opera shouted as he grabbed the bottom.

"'Cause it's hot air," Miguel explained. "That's what makes the big balloons float, too."

"That's why you use that burner thingie when you fly," I offered.

"You got it. Hot air always rises."

"If that's the case, why doesn't Vice Principal Watkins float off?" I asked.

Before Miguel could answer there was a loud ...

KWHOOOOOOSH!

I threw my head back to see a giant balloon slowly drift over our heads. "That's *your* balloon!" I exclaimed.

"Not mine," Miguel said as he shielded his eyes from the sun. "The markings are different."

"Hey, Mickey!" Three fellows shouted and waved from up in the basket.

Miguel hollered back, "Hi, guys!"

"Why weren't you flying today—it was beautiful!"

"Too much wind!" he shouted.

"Too much wind?" The tallest member of the group started to laugh. "More like too little courage!"

I could tell by the workout Miguel gave his jaw that they'd hit a nerve. But he played it cool. "We'll see about courage! You fellows still planning to race me Saturday?"

"Wouldn't miss it for the world," the tall one shouted, "unless, of course, you chicken out!" They were nearly out of view as they drifted over the trees on the other side of the parking lot. But you could still hear them laugh.

"I'll be there!" Mickey yelled after them, "Count on it!"

More laughter as they finally disappeared.

"Who are they?" Opera asked.

"Idiots," Miguel answered. "That tall guy with the mouth works for the other resort down the road. He's always bugging me."

"You guys have races?" I asked.

"All the time." Miguel nodded.

"Hey, maybe we could do that with you!" Opera exclaimed.

I shot him my strongest death glare. The type that says, "I hope you have a life-insurance policy or at least know a nearby hospital."

Finally, Miguel snapped off the hair dryer. Our little balloon was bulging at the seams and bucking to be let go. "Shall we do it?" he asked.

Opera and I nodded—and for good reason. If we hung on much longer we'd be joining those other guys in the sky!

"Okay," he ordered, "on my count. One . . . Two . . . Three!"

We let go of our balloon. It shot up like a rocket but didn't make a sound. Nothing. Total silence. Higher and higher it rose until it was over the tops of the trees. It's amazing, what a little hot air and paper could do—(plus whatever pieces of my shirt and Opera's hair that were still glued to it).

"You guys want to follow it?" Miguel asked.

"Sure!" we both exclaimed.

"Jump in the pickup and let's see where it goes!"

He didn't have to ask twice.

We hopped in the back and hung on for dear life as Miguel took off. Rocks and gravel flew in all directions as we spun out, hooting and hollering all the way.

Miguel drove like a madman as we bounced and skidded down dozens of different dirt roads trying to keep ahead of the balloon, trying to keep it in sight. I don't want to say Miguel was a reckless driver, but for a while I was beginning to think I wouldn't have to die in the balloon after all. Just a few more miles of riding with Miguel would do it.

Lots of times we lost the balloon behind trees, but Miguel always seemed to know where it would show up next.

"Isn't this fun?" Opera shouted. "Tomorrow that will be *us* up there. Just think of it!"

That's exactly what I was trying NOT to think of. And the only "fun" I had was knowing that the *balloon* was up in the air and *we* were down on the ground.

But Opera kept babbling about how in twenty-four hours that would be us up there . . . floating lazily in the breeze, drifting silently over the earth, blowing right into those . . .

HIGH VOLTAGE WIRES?

That's right. Before we knew it, the paper balloon hit some high voltage lines.

Miguel slammed on the brakes, and we all hopped out to watch.

In a matter of seconds, the balloon burst into flames. And our little pride and joy turned into our little pile of ashes.

"Oh, well." Opera shrugged as we climbed back in the pickup. "At least that's not us up there."

I gave him a look. He shrugged again. I glanced at my watch. It was nearly noon. I figured that gave me roughly eighteen hours. Eighteen hours left to live (if I survived the ride back). Eighteen hours. And then . . . well, then that *would* be us "up there."

Chapter 4

D–Day

It was colder than a church pew on Sunday morning.

Scarier than eating your little sister's cooking.

Darker than when you're out in the garage getting a tool for your dad when the light bulb's burned out. (Thanks, Dad, I just love risking my life for a Phillips head screwdriver.)

In short, I was not having a great time.

"Okay, Wally, Sis—on the count of three, we lift the bag out of the pickup and set it on the ground." Miguel was giving the orders. At least, I thought it was Miguel. At 5:00 in the morning it's hard to remember your own name, let alone anybody else's.

"Where's your friend Kenny?" Wall Street complained. "Why isn't he here to help?"

"Who needs Kenny, when I got you guys and Momma?" Miguel grinned. "Besides, he's fighting off the flu or something."

With enough grunts and groans (to let him know we sure missed ol' Kenny's presence), we pushed the heavy canvas bag to the edge of the pickup and kind of half set, half dropped it to the ground.

Miguel opened the top. There was nothing inside but folded cloth—lots and lots of folded cloth. "Okay," he said, "Opera, Wally—take this bag and walk it out as far as it will go."

"What is it?"

"It's the balloon. At least, it will be when we get it inflated."

Opera and I took hold of the bag and started pulling. The material spilled out as we walked farther and farther from the pickup. We were in a field. Don't worry, I already checked. The best I could see (which wasn't much in the dark) there were no bulls. Even if there were, no self-respecting bull would be up *this* early in the morning!

It all seemed so unfair—being dragged out of bed in the middle of the night just to die. At least in prison when they execute you at dawn, you don't have to build your own electric chair.

But here we were, up before the rest of civilization, unfolding a balloon, and getting ready for the ride of our lives . . . or deaths. In less than one hour we'd be going up. Which meant in less than an hour I'd be meeting God. Talk about unprepared.

I hadn't even brushed my teeth. Do you think they pass out Certs in heaven?

Then again, maybe things would work out. Maybe we'd be struck by a major earthquake, or maybe another outbreak of the Black Plague, or maybe they'd hurry up and build a railway right where I'm standing and hit me with a freight train. I should be so lucky.

"Wally?" Opera puffed as we kept pulling out the balloon. "You don't think we're going to land any-place outdoorsy, do you? I mean, where we have to hike, or anything like that?"

"Nah," I said, "this field is about as close to roughing it as you'll get."

"Good." He sighed. Then after another moment he started up again. "Wally?"

"Yeah, Opera?"

"I know you're really afraid of heights and worried about dying and everything." There was no missing the concern in his voice.

Good ol' Opera, a friend to the end.

"And I just want to say . . ." He paused for a second. Even in the dark I could tell my buddy was getting kind of choked up. "If that should happen . . ."

"You mean *when* it happens," I corrected. (Hey, if we're going for pity, let's go all the way.)

"When it happens . . . "

"Yes . . ."

"Boy, this is hard to say. . . . "

"Go ahead," I encouraged. "I know we're men, but it's okay to express our innermost feelings."

"Well then, if you should die . . ."

"Yes . . ."

" . . . could I have your CD player?"

Good ol' Opera, friend to the end.

The last of the balloon came out of the bag. But there was one minor problem. It had a ten-foot hole in the top!

"Uh . . . Miguel . . . *MIGUEL!*"

"Relax." Miguel laughed as he approached. In his hand was another big piece of material.

"What's that?" Opera asked.

"It's called a parachute," he said as he stooped down and began to lace it over the huge hole.

"*A parachute!*" I croaked.

"Don't worry, Wally. It's not a real parachute. We just use it to let the hot air out of the top."

" '*Let out?*' I thought the idea with hot air was '*to put it in*'?"

"Sure," Miguel chuckled, "until we want to land. And we do want to land, right?"

"We wouldn't have to worry about landing if we never took off," I offered.

They just looked at me. (Hey, you can't blame a guy for trying.)

Back at the truck we unloaded the wicker basket. Miguel set it on its side and attached the mouth of the balloon to it. Next he cranked up a gas-powered fan which started to fill the balloon with air. Soon it was full enough for him to step inside and walk around looking for rips or tears and stuff.

"Okay?" He grinned as he stepped back out. "Let's fire up the burner."

"Fire?" I moaned, vividly remembering the fate of our little model the day before.

He kneeled down to two giant silver burners attached to the top of the basket and pointed them toward the opening of the balloon.

"Momma, Sis—grab hold of the balloon's mouth and keep it pulled apart so the flame doesn't burn it."

"Are you sure this is safe?" his mom asked nervously.

"Momma," he assured her, "I do this all the time. Wally, Opera—once I get this thing fired up, you'll need to run back down to the top of the balloon and hold down the crown line. As it fills with heat, it'll want to roll back and forth."

"Gotcha."

He adjusted a few valves and suddenly . . .

KWOOOOOOSH! . . . there was that old familiar sound—accompanied by a six-foot-long flame shooting into the balloon. Wall Street gave a little scream and almost let go of the opening.

"Hold it open, Sis! Hold it open!"

She and Momma obeyed as the flame shot into the balloon, filling it with the fiery hot air.

Opera and I raced down to the other end as fast as we could and grabbed the rope connected to the top of the balloon. In a matter of minutes, the balloon started rolling back and forth just like Miguel had said. At first it wasn't much. But pretty soon it turned into a real wrestling match.

"Hold it steady!" Miguel shouted. "Hold it down with that crown line."

"I can't hang on!" Opera shouted as the balloon rolled back and forth. "The line keeps slipping from my hands!"

I, on the other hand, wrapped the rope around my hand good and tight. I mean *good and tight*. No way would I let it slip away from me.

The good news was it didn't. The bad news was I did. Not from the balloon, but from the ground. As the balloon whipped back and forth, it started yanking my arm back and forth. And since my arm and I are kinda attached, it yanked me back and forth, too!

"Let go!" Opera shouted, "Wally, let go!"

"I CAN'T! I struggled with the rope as the balloon kept throwing me around and rising higher and higher.

"You're supposed to ride *under* the balloon," Opera shouted, "not on *top* of it!"

"Thanks for the reminder," I shouted back.

Then, when I was positive that I would forever be attached to the balloon, that I had become the first human blimp (and wondered if that meant I could see all the Super Bowl games for free), my hand slipped from the rope.

I hit the ground with a soggy . . .

KERSPLAT!

It would have been a . . .

KERTHUMP! . . . but by luck I found the only cow pie in the entire field. At least I thought it was a cow pie. It sure smelled like a cow pie. But in two minutes and thirty four seconds I'd find out this pie didn't exactly belong to a "cow."

"Keep the rope tight!" Miguel shouted. "As the balloon fills, let it out—walk her back till she's up over the basket!"

It was quite a fight, but between the two of us, we managed. Soon the balloon hovered over the basket.

Miguel had already climbed in. "Okay everybody," he shouted over the roar of the burner, "come on board!"

Opera and Wall Street quickly scampered into the basket. I would have joined them, but I was busy shoving my glasses up on my nose and saying a little prayer.

"Momma," Miguel shouted. "You sure you know how to drive a pickup?"

"Since before you were born!" She tried to look brave, but there was no missing the worry in her eyes.

"Come on, Wally!" Miguel shouted. "We're nearly ready!"

"Huh? Oh, yeah, uh . . . right." I glanced around. Fortunately, I noticed something important had to be done—like retying my shoes.

The basket gave a little scoot on the ground.

"Get in!" Miguel shouted. "Now! We're almost airborne!"

I stood up. Well, it was now or never (unfortunately the "never" part wasn't much of an option). I did my best imitation of an athlete as I threw one leg over the basket and tried to climb in. Well, so much for imitations. I got hung up. One foot was in, the other foot was still hanging out. I kicked my inside foot around and only succeeded in getting it tangled up in some sort of a bungee cord that was coiled up and hanging inside.

"Miguel, I'm stuck."

"Quit horsing around." He scowled. I could tell he was getting pretty serious.

"I'm not kidding," I said, "I'm really—"

"Wait a minute!" Opera shouted. "I forgot our lunch!"

"NO OPERA, STAY IN THE—"

But before Miguel could finish the warning, Opera had leaped out of the basket . . . which meant the basket was suddenly a whole lot lighter . . . which meant we started to rise!

"GRAB HOLD OF THE SIDES! MOMMA, OPERA, GRAB HOLD OF THE SIDES! HOLD US DOWN!"

They did. Together Opera and Momma managed to pull us back down . . . a little. I would have helped, but I was still caught on the edge.

And then we heard it:

Mooo . . .

Everyone spun around to the sound. But there were too many bushes to see clearly.

MooooOOOO . . .

Wall Street stuttered. "You . . . you don't think that's a—"

"Don't be stupid," Opera chided. "That's a cow if ever I heard one."

"Uh, guys . . ." I interrupted, "I'm still kind of hung up here."

"Opera, climb in the basket," Miguel demanded.

But Opera and Wall Street were suddenly in the middle of what they did best. Arguing.

"How would you know the difference between a bull and a cow?" Wall Street demanded. "You've lived your whole life in the city."

"Hey, I watch PBS!"

"Opera, climb in the basket now or we're going to—"

MOOOOOOO . . .

"Uh, guys, could one of you give me a hand here . . ."

MOOOOOOOOOO . . .

"It sounds like a bull to me," Wall Street insisted.

"Uh, guys . . ."

"If it's a bull it would be charging by now," Opera said as he threw a look over his shoulder. "And as you can clearly see, there's nothing heading toward us but . . ."

Finally the "cow" came into view. Its head was lowered, and it was charging.

"*. . . A BULL!!!*" Opera shouted. In his panic he momentarily let go of the basket.

"NO!" Miguel cried. "JUMP BACK IN, DON'T LET—!"

He was too late. The balloon gave a giant leap.

Wall Street screamed and in a desperate panic scampered over the edge of the basket and leaped out, too.

"NO!" Miguel shouted, "DON'T—"

But again he was too late. Opera and Momma tried to hang on but the balloon was too strong. It started to rise.

The bull continued his charge.

"LET GO!" Miguel shouted. "RUN TO THE TRUCK!"

"But—"

"LET GO! WE'LL BE ALL RIGHT!"

The bull was nearly there, and by the look of things he'd already picked out his target. But it wasn't Opera or Wall Street or Momma. It wasn't even the basket. It was who or what was hanging over the basket. That's right, ol' bully decided my rear end was going to be his next bull's eye!

The balloon gave another lunge and finally ripped out of Opera's and Momma's hands, sending Miguel and me shooting high up into the sky.

The only problem was, when we shot up, I shot out!

"AUGHHHHHHHHHH . . ." I screamed as I tumbled out of the basket.

The ground was twenty feet below. But I only fell about six feet before I bounced back up, then fell again, then bounced back up, then fell. *What's going on?* I thought. *Can't I even do a simple thing like fall to my death?* Then I noticed the pain around my ankle. The best I could figure the bungee cord that was tangled around my foot had tightened. It was the only thing stopping me from becoming a human omelet on the pasture below.

As I bounced past the loose end of the cord, I grabbed it and held on tight . . . hoping that the *other* end was fastened to the basket.

I looked up. There was Miguel, holding on to the bungee cord as if his life depended on it. (Actually it was *my* life that depended on it.) I appreciated his effort, but I wasn't crazy about this hanging upside down business or about bouncing up and down like a human yo-yo.

The balloon kept rising, Miguel kept holding on, and I kept bouncing. They say great minds think the clearest in times of trouble. And I was proof of the theory.

"OPERA!" I screamed.

"Yeah?" his voice drifted up from somewhere under the truck.

"The CD player is yours!"

Chapter 5

A Little God Talk

"Wally . . . Wally, open your eyes . . . Wally?"

The last time I saw the ground it was upside down and about a 30 yards farther away than it should have been. It was then that I decided to do what any All-American Coward would do. I had shut my eyes.

That had been ten minutes ago.

Somehow Miguel had managed to pull me into the basket where I was now huddled in a corner against one of the fuel tanks, kind of half shuddering, half shivering . . . but mostly half dying.

"C'mon, Wally," Miguel urged, "you can't keep your eyes shut forever."

I answered, "If I open my eyes, it means I'm awake . . . and if I'm awake, it means I'm not dreaming. And if I'm not dreaming, I'm in big trouble."

He chuckled as he shut off the burner. Suddenly everything became silent. *Real* silent. "You're missing a beautiful sunrise," he said.

What did I care about sunrises? Any second we were going to die, and I was going to meet God with a bad case of morning breath!

Yet everything was so still and quiet it seemed like we hadn't risen an inch. Maybe I'd just get by with a broken arm then . . . or a leg or a neck. Maybe it would be okay to sneak one quick little peek. . . .

Summoning up all my McDoogle courage, I opened my eyes.

Miguel was right. It was beautiful. And peaceful. In fact, it was so incredibly still I thought maybe I'd already died and gone to heaven.

"Hey," I asked, looking down over the basket, "where are the trees?"

Below us was a blanket of soft, swirling cotton— but a blanket that glowed with the fiery reds and oranges of the sunrise. It was like we were in a strange and incredible world. But a world without trees.

"The trees are 900 feet below us," Miguel explained.

"900 FEET!"

"Yeah, just underneath those clouds down there."

"Those are clouds?" I cried, pointing down to the cotton blanket. "What are they doing there? They're supposed to be above us!"

Miguel chuckled again. "Relax, Wally—enjoy it. There's nothing in the world like this."

He had a point. Even in my nail-chomping frenzy there was something so soothing, so peaceful . . . and, above all, so quiet. No sound, no movement, only stillness. Pretty soon even I started to relax.

"Guess we better radio the truck," Miguel said as he pulled out one of the walkie-talkies. "Let Momma know where we're heading."

I glanced around the basket. There was no steering wheel, no rudder, no nothing. Only three little gauges and the burner above our head. "How do you steer this thing?" I asked.

"You don't."

Suddenly I wasn't so relaxed.

"You just gotta go with the wind," he explained, ". . . wherever it takes you."

"But how do you know where?" I asked. "It doesn't even feel like we're moving."

"That's what these gauges are for. You can't go by your feelings up here. You have to trust those gauges." He clicked on the walkie-talkie. "Mickey to Momma, Mickey to Momma—do you read me?"

There was nothing on the other end but static.

He pointed back to the gauges in front of us. "That one tells our height, that's the temperature, and that's our rate of climbing or falling."

There was that word again . . . *falling*.

He continued. "By adjusting our altitude with the burner, we can rise into or drop out of different wind currents. And since each wind current travels a different direction . . ."

"We can control our direction," I finished.

"You got it. By traveling up and down, we actually end up steering this thing." Again he clicked the talk key. "Mickey to Momma, Mickey to Momma—you guys hear us?"

More static, then a familiar and very worried voice. "Mickey, Mickey is that you? Where are you, sweetheart?"

Miguel broke into a smile. "Hello, Momma. We're about three miles due east of the launch site. Get back on Highway 34. Head east six miles. There's a parking lot in back of a gas station and a Seven-Eleven—you passed it driving up here. We'll try to set down there."

After a few more nervous questions at the Momma end and plenty of It'll-be-okays from the Miguel end, he finally turned off the radio.

"Why do you keep this bungee cord?" I asked as I began to rewind it. It was a lot longer than I had thought.

"I keep it around for fun." He grinned.

My eyes widened. "Don't tell me you bungee jump along with everything else?"

"You should try it, Wally," he laughed, "it will change your life."

"You could say the same thing about dying," I said.

He smiled again and continued, "There's a whole world out there, Wally. I just want to live it. I want to taste and see and do and try *everything* . . . and bungee jumping, that's part of it." Suddenly, he pointed below, "Look at that!"

A giant eagle crested through the tops of the clouds. He skimmed above the surface slowly and majestically. His gigantic wings and broad back looked strong enough for a person to ride on. Don't worry, I wasn't about to try it. And luckily Miguel hadn't thought of it . . . yet.

Finally the mighty bird dipped his left wing and disappeared back into the blanket of clouds.

"Wow!" I exclaimed.

Miguel agreed. "I tell you, when you're up in this silence, surrounded by all this beauty . . . it's almost enough to make a guy believe there really is a God."

"*Almost?*" I asked, glancing at him.

He smiled. "You been talking to Sis?"

"A little . . ."

"She's pretty bummed about my leaving and stuff, isn't she?"

"Confused, mostly."

He nodded. "Me, too."

I wanted to say something. You know, some speech about how much God loves him. How, even though he's left, he can come back to Jesus again. But I was too scared. Wally McDoogle, Super Chicken, struck again. The only thing I could do was squeak out a pathetic little, "Why . . . why are you confused?"

"Got me . . ." He let out a long sigh. "I guess when Dad left I just started wondering if I could believe in anything anymore . . . even God."

More silence. Lots of it.

After a moment, Miguel continued. "If I can't see Him, or touch Him, I figure how do I know God's even real?"

More silence. Boy, could I argue or what? I was really laying into this poor guy.

He let out another sigh. "Of course, I guess you can say the same thing about the wind . . . I mean we can't see it or touch it either . . . but it sure has an effect on us doesn't it?"

I nodded. He'd put the words right in my mouth.

*   *   *   *   *

About an hour later, Miguel slowly eased the balloon down in the Seven-Eleven parking lot just like he had predicted. It was a lot smoother landing than the take off. Everyone greeted us and slapped us on the back . . . well, everyone but the bull.

Wall Street and Opera were pretty jealous. Being the good friend I was . . . (and wanting to show my thanks for all their help at take off), I did my best to rub it in.

I was feeling pretty good (who says revenge isn't sweet), until Miguel stepped in. "Maybe you guys would like to come up with me again tomorrow?"

"Really?" they shouted.

"Sure," he said, "but you're going to have to listen a lot better than you did this morning."

Everyone quickly agreed.

"Great," he grinned. "Beause I can't think of a better crew to help me with my race tomorrow."

"Race?" Wall Street cried. "We get to be in your race?"

"Did you hear that?" Opera shouted to me. "Isn't that great? You get to do this all over again!"

I pretended to smile but was actually checking my pockets for change. I'd be swinging by the Seven-Eleven convenience store to pick up a package of breath mints. Surviving one balloon flight was one thing. But for someone with my luck to live through two . . . well, I was definitely going to look and smell my best when I met God.

* * * * *

After dinner I whipped out ol' Betsy to finish my
Ecology-Man story. I mean, what is worse than
having a half finished story lying around when
you're dead?

Now, where we? Oh, yeah . . .

Toxoid Breath is doing his best to
suffocate our goodest of good guys. But
not with morning breath, not with the
smell of stale corn chips, not even with
the deadly aroma of gym socks left all
semester in his locker. No, Toxoid
Breath is about to smother Ecology-Man
with . . . Da-da-daaaa! (that's bad guy
music) . . . Air Pollution!

But Ecology-Man has a solution to the
pollution. He throws back his head and
cries:

"Oh, winds, come hither to assist
your humble servant in his never-
ending (and politically correct)
war against pollution!"

Everyone waits with baited breath.
(How you get "baited breath" is beyond

me. Unless you stick out your tongue at a bunch of fishermen and one of them grabs it and wraps worms around it and tosses it into the lake. Who knows. Who cares. Back to our story . . .)

Suddenly a tornado roars down from the clouds. But it's no ordinary tornado. This one learned to talk by watching TV. Unfortunately it only gets MTV, so its style is more rap than talk . . .

"Yo, Enviro-Dude,
How y'all doin',
It's been a long time,
So tell me what's a brewin'?"

"Wendell, you old windbag," Ecology-Man shouts, "is that really you?"

"None other—give me five, Bro."

They high five (no easy trick with a tornado).

"How's Wendy, your wife?" Ecology-Man asks, "and your little gusts, Stormy and Breezy?"

"The wife's jus' fine,
The kids are really growin'.
Shootin' up like whirlwinds,
a puffin and a blowin'."

Before Wendell can show pictures of
the kids or play home videos of their
latest vacation to Disney World, the
dreaded Toxoid Breath reaches to his
iron belly and pulls another lever.

A giant door hisses open. There,
standing alone on the platform in all
of his glory is . . . Kirby, the vacuum
cleaner salesman.

"Hi, there," he calls. "Can I interest
you in this year's new and improve—"

"Not now, Bro.
We're catchin' up on life.
Come back tomorrow,
and talk to the wife."

"But it'll only take a minute. All I
have to do is flip this switch and—"

Suddenly the vacuum cleaner roars to
life. It starts sucking up everything in
its path—ground-in-dirt, dust in those
hard-to-reach places, leaves, trees
connected to those leaves (hey, these
machines are powerful), and finally ol'
Wendell, himself.

Ecology-Man grabs a boulder and hangs
on with his manly hands. But not Wendell.

(As we all know, tornadoes are a little short in the hands department.) He screams for help as his funnel cloud is drawn into the vacuum's nozzle. "Ecology-Man . . . Help me! Help me!"

But there's little our hero (and part-time life-insurance agent) can do . . . except sell another policy. "Hey, Wendell, have you thought of increasing your coverage? Looks like you might need it."

The tornado has little time to answer (let alone write a check). Quicker than you can turn to see how many pages this goes on, Wendell is sucked into the vacuum cleaner!

SLUUUUUUUUUUUP GULP Ahhhh . . .

"Wendell!" Ecology-Man screams at the vacuum cleaner. "Can you hear me?"

There is no sound from the machine except a muffled *burp* . . .

Now our hero is mad . . . really mad. Madder than when his dad chewed up his Leggos in the lawn mower. Madder than when he missed his favorite TV shows because every channel had election returns. Almost as mad as when Collision, his sister's cat, ate too much grass and threw

up in his left tennis shoe without bother-
ing to tell him so when he slipped his
foot into it in the morning. . . . Well,
you probably get the picture. . . .

But Toxoid Breath isn't finished. He
forces the vacuum cleaner salesman to
switch his machine to "High" and aim it
directly at our gorgeously good-looking
good guy.

Ecology-Man hangs on to his boulder
for dear life as . . .

Off come his shoes . . .

Off come his socks . . .

Off come his pants . . .

Now it is just our hero in his Beauty-
and-the-Beast boxer shorts. But just
before they start to slip away, our
radically recyclable hero shouts—

"Come on guys." It was Miguel's voice. He
was knocking on our room door. "Got a big day,
tomorrow. Turn off the light and get some
shuteye."

I threw a look over to Opera. He was already
counting sheep. Better make that Twinkies snack
cakes. Yeah, by the smile on his face it was definitely Twinkies.

With a heavy sigh, I shut ol' Betsy down. As much as I hated leaving a story half finished, I knew I had to be alert for tomorrow. The last thing I wanted to do was nod off and doze through my own death.

Chapter 6

Going Up?

"No pressure," Miguel whispered as we unloaded the balloon from the pickup the following morning. "But if those guys over there beat us, I'll be humiliated for life!"

"Thanks," I sighed as I glanced over to the other team. "That sure takes a load off my mind."

"You have a mind?" Wall Street smirked.

Everyone snickered. Everyone but Momma. She just stood beside the truck doing what she did best . . . looking worried. She would have joined in the conversation, but she'd already covered her list of topics:

"Are you sure it's safe?"
"Are you really sure it's safe?"
"Are you really really sure it's safe?"
"Are you really really really . . . "
(Well, you get the picture.)

Miguel promised her everything would be fine—
that we'd be safer in the air than she'd be driving
on the ground. Of course, she nodded and pretended to believe him . . . but of course, she didn't.

"Hey, Mickey!" It was the tall guy from the other
team. The one with the big mouth. He was unload-
ing their balloon from their truck. "Sure you don't
want to chicken out? Feels like there might be a
teensy-weensy little breeze starting."

There was no missing his sarcasm, but he had
a point. A small wind had picked up.

"Don't pay any attention to him," Miguel muttered.

But the Mouth continued, "After we clean your
clocks, the least you and the kiddies can do is
swing by the resort and wash our truck."

"No need," Miguel shot back. "After we trounce
you, you'll be too humiliated to be seen in public!"

It wasn't much of a comeback, but considering
his chances of winning, it wasn't too bad. I mean,
look who he had to work with. The four of us were
definitely the losingest bunch of winners I'd ever
seen.

—First there was me, with my fear of heights.

—Then Opera, with his fear of the great outdoors.

—And don't forget Wall Street, with her fear of
   losing her brother.

—And, of course, Momma, with her fear of . . .
everything.

Yes sir, we were definitely world-class, cham-
pion, triple-A Losers. But that didn't seem to
bother Miguel. He went right on working with us
like we were pros.

A half hour later the balloons were up and inflated. Both teams fought to hold their bucking
baskets in place as the Mouth shouted last-minute
instructions:

"Basket weights look the same—three men in
ours . . . three kiddies and half a man in yours."

His group gave the usual sneers and laughs.

He continued, "Closest one to the marker in old
man Wilson's field is the winner, right?"

Miguel nodded as he fired another burst of
flame into our balloon. Momma held onto the basket as Opera, Wall Street, and yours truly climbed
on board.

"On my count," Mouth shouted.

Again Miguel nodded. The balloon started to
buck. More than yesterday. A lot more. The wind
had definitely picked up.

"Mickey—" I started to ask.

"It'll be fine," he cut me off. "Everything's fine."

I wanted to argue, but with the pressure he was
getting from the guys, I figured it wouldn't do any
good. Besides he was the expert. Then there was

his mom. The look on her face said she had enough to worry about already.

"Okay, Momma," he said. "When he says 'three,' let go."

She nodded.

I prayed.

"One . . . " Mouth shouted.

Miguel reached over and tapped one of the gauges.

I prayed harder.

"Two . . . "

He re-checked his fuel tanks.

I prayed even harder.

"Three!"

Miguel fired the burner, Momma let go of the basket, and we were off! The burners roared as everyone hooted and hollered. Well, everyone but me. I was too busy popping breath mints into my mouth—one after another after another.

At first, everything went smoothly.

"This is incredible!" Opera cried.

"Fantastic!" Wall Street agreed.

Being the seasoned pro, I pretended to yawn. Then I spotted a little sandbag with a yellow flag tied to it. "What's this?" I asked.

"That's what we hit the marker in Old Man Wilson's field with."

"I thought you said it was a race!"

"It is—only with balloons you don't race for speed, you race for accuracy. The closest one to hit the marker is the winner."

Suddenly the balloon gave a little shudder . . . then a bigger bump.

"What was that?" In all my experience of ballooning (some forty-two minutes and sixteen seconds from yesterday) I had never felt anything but smooth floating.

Again the balloon shuddered . . . harder this time. Then we started turning. Slowly at first. Then faster and faster.

"Miguel!?" Wall Street cried.

His eyes shot to the gauges. "It's a thermal!"

"A what?" Wall Street shouted.

"A bubble of hot air—it's taking us up!" He looked toward the balloon as it gave another shudder and started to shake. We followed his gaze and, in perfect three-part harmony, gasped.

The balloon was caving in!

Quickly, Miguel fired the burner over our heads. "What are you doing!" Wall Street cried.

"I'm taking us up!"

"We want *down*, not *up!*" Wall Street screamed.

"No way!" he shouted over the roar of the burner. "We've got to keep the bag filled!"

As the bumping and spinning increased we began to sway back and forth.

"Hang on!" Miguel shouted.

The balloon gave another lunge, and we all screamed—again in perfect harmony. (I couldn't help thinking we should take our act on the road, maybe pick up a recording contract, make a music video—)

"Miguel," Wall Street cried, "Get us out of this! Get us down!"

"The only way out is up! We gotta ride this thing to the top!"

More spinning and swinging.

"How high?" Opera shouted.

"What?"

"How high will it take us??"

"No telling—at this rate, a few thousand feet!"

"A FEW THOUSAND FEET!" I cried.

The balloon gave another jarring bounce, followed by even more rocking.

It was wilder than any carnival ride I'd ever been on (not that there's a lot of action on the merry-go-round). It was almost as bad as when Dad taught Brock to drive in the Wal-Mart parking lot! Luckily, up here, there were no shopping carts to hit . . . let alone light poles . . . or garbage dumpsters . . . or little old ladies. (Don't worry, last we heard she was recovering nicely.)

But there was another problem—the one dealing with our bodies and the basket, more precisely with keeping our bodies from being thrown out of the basket!

"Okay, everybody scoot down!"

"WHAT?" we shouted.

"Sit down! To be safe, everybody sit down!"

We quickly dropped to the floor of the basket as it kept rocking and swaying. All we could see now was the balloon . . . and believe me, that was enough. It was pretty scary watching the giant bag twist and snap and expand and collapse.

Then, as quickly as it started, it stopped. The balloon filled out, and we were back to normal. Oh, there were a few little bumps and turns, just to remind us what a good time we'd had, but basically the white-knuckled fun was over.

Finally, Miguel glanced down to us and nodded. We crawled back to our feet and looked over the edge.

Not a good idea.

Ever seen one of those pictures NASA takes of Earth from outer space? It could have been taken from our balloon. I don't want to say we were high, but we all kept ducking our heads just to make sure we didn't bump into the moon.

"You said there wouldn't be any problem!" Wall Street accused. She was practically in tears. "You said this would be safe!"

"You're still alive, aren't you?" Miguel snapped. "I don't see any bleeding—no broken bones."

He had a point. Other than a few extra million gray hairs, we all looked pretty much the same.

Now it was time to get serious. Now it was time to evaluate our problem and ask the important questions. Opera took the lead. "So . . . do you think we'll be back in time for lunch?"

Miguel gave him a look. "I just hope we'll be back, period."

"What . . . what do you mean?" I asked.

"That little thermal drove us up so high and fast, there's no telling what direction the winds below us are heading.

"That's bad?"

"It just means I don't know where we'll land."

"That's bad."

With that bit of cheery news we all kinda huddled together in silence as Miguel pulled on the rope leading up to the "parachute."

"I'm letting hot air out of the top," he volunteered, "so we can get back down and land."

I looked over the edge of the basket. "Land where?" I asked. "There's nothing below us but mountains—miles and miles of mountains."

Opera gave a hearty gulp. "Not to mention a few grizzlies, cougars, wolves and—"

"Yeah, yeah, we get the picture," Wall Street cut him off. Turning to her brother she asked, "But you have some idea where we'll land, right—I mean, like a general idea?"

"Yeah," Opera asked hopefully. "Like near a Motel 6, or a McDonald's, or—"

"Sorry, guys." Miguel shrugged as he worked the rope.

Uh-oh.

"I don't have a clue . . . "

·Double uh-oh.

So there we were . . . Miguel and three city slickers, a zillion miles above the earth, dropping into winds that blew in who-knew-what-direction so we could land in who-knew-what-location. Yes sir, another fun-filled day in the life of Wally McDoogle.

I offered Opera my last mint and wondered who'd get my CD now that we were both checking into heaven together.

Chapter 7

Going Down?

The next couple of hours were pretty boring. I mean, once you know the "how" of how you're going to die, and the "where" of where you're going to die, it gets kinda monotonous sitting around waiting for the "when."

To help pass time, Opera and I figured we'd have a major argument on the subject. He was sure we were going to die when we became some grizzly bear's dinner. I, being the optimist, insisted that once we smashed into the ground at a trillion miles an hour there wouldn't be enough of us left for any animal to nibble on.

Meanwhile, Wall Street just kept staring over the edge. No way could she see her mom from where we were. There was nothing but trees and mountains. But I guess she had nothing better to do.

The only one who wasn't bored was Miguel. When he wasn't searching for the right air current, he was trying to contact his mom on the walkie-talkie.

Unfortunately, he didn't have much luck in either department.

"We're out of range for the radios." He sighed as he pulled the parachute to drop us down into another current. An air current that he hoped would take us west and toward home.

Of course it took us east and away from everything.

"How long can we stay up here?" Wall Street asked.

"We got plenty of fuel," he said, motioning toward the tanks fastened to the inside of the basket. "But the winds are working against us—the longer we stay up the farther we drift into the wilderness."

"*Wilderness?*" Opera croaked.

"The best I can figure, the nearest town is fifty miles."

"*Fifty miles?*" Opera exclaimed. He was beginning to sound like an echo.

Miguel nodded. "Hey, check it out," he said pointing off to the right. "Down there on the ridge—it looks like a logging road."

"*A logging road?*" Opera repeated for no reason except it was getting to be a habit.

We all looked. It wasn't much, but with the miles and miles of trees anything that wasn't green was of interest.

Miguel carefully surveyed the horizon. "There's nothing else in sight—no fields, no nothing. It looks like we'll have to take our chances and set down on that road."

"But . . ." Opera looked a little worried. "I don't see any Burger King, or Taco Bell, or Kentucky Fried—"

"It'll have to do," Miguel interrupted, "or they'll never find us." He pulled the parachute rope again. More air escaped and we dropped a little faster. We started to twist and turn, but not nearly as bad as before.

"This is going to get tricky," Miguel said. "The way those trees are blowing, it looks like we got ourselves quite a ground wind."

"What does that mean?" I asked.

"It's going to be a fight to land on the road and not in the treetops."

We all looked down and watched as we came closer and closer to our brand new enemies. Don't get me wrong, treetops look great with twinkle lights, Christmas ornaments, and angels stuck on top . . . but somehow we suspected they wouldn't look so great when jammed through the middle of a balloon basket.

Carefully, Miguel edged the balloon toward the road . . . trying to outguess the wind, hoping it would push us in the right direction. Closer and closer we came.

Suddenly there was a scraping sound against the basket. "What's that?" I shouted.

"Treetops," Opera called as he leaned over the edge. "We're brushing against treetops."

"Don't lean out!" Miguel shouted. "Keep your balance!"

He fired the burner again. We lifted up slightly and continued to drift until we were clear of the trees and finally over the road. Quickly Miguel let out more air. We dropped below the treetops and headed in for a perfect landing.

Everything was fine until we were hit with another gust of wind. The balloon picked up speed. The road was just a few feet below us, but we couldn't seem to drop down to it; instead, we kept racing above it!

"Bend your knees!" he shouted. "We're going to hit hard!" He yanked on the parachute.

The ground came up fast.

"When we hit don't stiffen!" Miguel shouted. "Go limp! Just let your bodies—"

But that was as far as he got.

K—R A S H

The balloon hit. But it wasn't the crash that threw us. It was the:

SCRAPE . . . SLIDE . . . SLIDE . . . SCRAPE . . .

that got our attention. Even though we had stopped going down we hadn't stopped going forward. We were still racing down the road—only instead of above it, we were bouncing and sliding *on it!*

Miguel yanked the parachute rope with all his might, but it did little good. We just kept scooting. Then the basket hit one too many bumps and tipped over. I was thrown out. Opera and Wall Street followed. Each of us rolled and skidded across the ground. "Ouch!" "Ooo!" "Boy does that smart!"

But the basket kept going. So did Miguel. He was still inside, hanging on for dear life . . . and heading directly for a stand of trees!

"GET UP HERE!" he shouted back to us. "RUN UP HERE AND GRAB THE BASKET!"

We scrambled to our feet. Opera and I were in the lead. We raced toward Miguel for all we were worth. We were pretty bruised and scratched, but we didn't feel the pain—not yet.

Unfortunately, Miguel wasn't so lucky. The balloon kept dragging the basket, which kept knocking him around. But he wouldn't let go of the parachute rope. Not for the world.

"HURRY, GUYS!"

At last we caught up and lunged for the basket. Opera caught hold of it. But all I caught was a handful of air . . . until I hit the ground. Then it was a mouthful of dirt.

Opera hung on. He sat down, sliding along on his rear as Miguel was tossed and bounced around inside like a pinball.

"MICKEY!" Wall Street screamed as she raced past me.

I leaped to my feet and followed. Slowly the balloon began to collapse until finally the basket came to a stop.

"MICKEY!" Wall Street cried as she arrived beside him. "MICKEY!"

"I'm all right, Sis—I'm all right . . ."

But he wasn't all right. One look at the side of his head, his scraped stomach and his twisted leg proved that.

"Jump on the balloon," he gasped, "don't let it blow away!"

Wall Street refused to leave his side, but Opera and I ran to the half-inflated balloon which was lying on the ground. We leaped into the giant air bag with all of our might, forcing out more of the air.

"Don't rip it!" Miguel shouted. "We might need . . ." But that was all he said.

"MICKEY!" Wall Street screamed. "MICKEY!" We spun around to the basket.

Miguel was sprawled out on the ground beside it. He wasn't moving.

"*M I C K E Y !*"

*   *   *   *   *

"I can't believe it," I said to Opera as we dragged another broken branch to the campfire. "It's almost dark, and you still haven't been eaten by a bear or skunk or ground hog or nothin'."

Opera scowled. "Laugh all you want, but the night's still young."

The group gave a little chuckle.

It was the first time any of us had laughed since the crash, and it felt pretty good. Despite the wind whipping over the ridge, we'd managed to build a pretty good fire. In fact, over the last few hours, we'd managed to set up a pretty good camp. I mean, if you worked at it, you could almost convince yourself we were on a little vacation. Of course, it would have been more convincing if we had cable TV, a spa, and maybe some room service. But at least we were alive.

And that went for Miguel, too. For someone who was supposed to be dead, he was doing a pretty good imitation of being okay. Well, except for the broken leg, the concussion, and whatever else was wrong.

"Don't try to move me," he had ordered when he finally came to. "I think something's busted inside." He coughed hard and winced in pain. "You'd better leave me here, stationary."

So instead of dragging him off to the campsite, we built the campsite beside him—right in the middle of the road. But that was okay. With all the overgrown weeds we figured there hadn't been a major rush hour in, oh, the last ten to twenty years.

"They'll send up search planes at sunrise," Miguel explained as he fiddled with the walkie-talkies. The radios seemed to work, but there was nobody in range to talk to.

"How will anybody find us way out here?" I asked.

"Oh, they'll find us." He coughed. "Maybe in two or three days, but they'll find us."

"But you're hurt," Wall Street blurted out. "You need medical help *now*."

Miguel shrugged.

"You're the expert!" she practically shouted. (Once she knew he was alive, I guess she figured it was okay to be mad at him again.) "We just can't sit around and watch you as you . . ." She couldn't finish the thought, but we all knew what it was.

After a nervous kind of silence I jumped in. "Couldn't we walk back?"

"Not on this road," Miguel explained. "The way it winds and turns it would take forever."

"So what do we do?" Wall Street demanded. Her voice was getting kinda thin and shaky.

Miguel looked to the ground and stared real hard. We waited, but we knew he didn't have an answer. No one said a word. The silence grew longer and more uneasy. Then we heard it . . .

A low growl.

We looked at each other.

"Do you hear that?" I whispered.

"Shhhh . . ."

There was another one.

"What is it?" Wall Street whispered.

"I wouldn't worry about it," Opera said.

We all spun to him. For being King of the Outdoor Cowards he sounded pretty brave.

There was another growl, even louder.

"What do you think we should do?" I asked.

Opera gave a sheepish grin . . . "Just find me something to eat—that's my stomach growling."

We all groaned. He shrugged.

Silence again fell upon our little group. Except for the crackling fire, Miguel's occasional fits of coughing, and Opera's intestinal rumblings, there wasn't a sound. We all knew how bleak things looked.

Finally Opera spoke up. "Maybe we should, you know, pray."

"Pray?" Miguel asked.

"Well, yeah . . ."

"A lot of good praying did us," Wall Street sulked.

"What do you mean?" I asked.

She answered, "You're afraid of heights . . . so we get caught in a major thermal. Opera's afraid of the outdoors . . . so here we are, outdoors. Mickey doesn't believe God loves him . . . so he proves it by nearly killing him."

"Maybe that's why all this is happening," Opera ventured. We all looked at him. He shrugged again. "I mean, maybe God wants to prove that He answers prayer by putting us all in a place like this where He can."

For some reason it seemed to make sense—at least to me. I couldn't help giving a little smile. It's nice to know that sometimes Opera has more between his ears than some new snack food.

"He might have a point," I offered. "I mean, isn't that what Pastor Bergman's always going on about? That we're supposed to trust God even when everything around us says He's wrong?"

Wall Street sighed in frustration. She'd had enough unanswered prayers—she wasn't in the mood for any more.

"No, seriously," I continued. "Opera's afraid of the great outdoors, so God puts him here to prove He'll protect him. I'm afraid of heights, so here I am. Wall Street doesn't know if she can trust God . . . and Miguel doesn't even know if there is a God. Think of it—I mean, what a perfect place for us all to find out."

Wall Street stared into the fire like maybe I might have a point, but she wouldn't admit it.

Miguel just looked at me and broke into a little smile. "Maybe you should give up writing and be a preacher, McDoogle."

I grinned back. He was right. It was a pretty cool sermon. I wasn't sure I believed it, but it was definitely cool.

Another pause. More stomach growling. More coughing.

"So . . ." Opera hedged, "are we going to pray or what?"

"Why not," Miguel finally shrugged, "if you're sure He can hear us over all that noise your stomach's making."

Everyone snickered. Then finally, slowly we all got around to bowing our heads. Nobody wanted to start. Least of all me. But if I didn't, I knew we'd probably stay that way forever, so I jumped in to kick things off.

As far as prayers go, it was pretty good. Even Wall Street managed to eke out a little something. Of course, Miguel didn't say a word, but that was no surprise. Opera finally ended it with, " . . . and please Lord, if possible, help us find somebody's leftover picnic basket." We all chuckled and threw in a few extra "amen"s. But when we looked up we saw Miguel staring at the fire kinda funny like.

"Listen, uh," he cleared his throat, "this is kinda weird . . .

He started coughing again. We exchanged worried glances.

" . . . but when you were praying I had an idea." We waited.

Finally he looked up. "I know a way we can be spotted tomorrow."

"How's that?" Wall Street asked.

"Tie down the balloon and send one of you up above the treetops in it."

"Do what?" we all asked in our famous three part harmony.

"Yeah," Miguel was getting excited, which meant a little more coughing. Finally, he finished and continued. "Take that 200-foot bungee cord I have in the basket, tie the balloon down good and tight with it, and send one of you up above the trees." He coughed a couple more times. "It'll be a little rough in this wind, but once you're up, any plane in twenty miles will be able to spot you."

"That's a great idea," I said glancing around the group, "but who?"

"To conserve fuel, it has to be the lightest one."

Suddenly his idea wasn't so great. Suddenly it stunk. Quickly I puffed out my cheeks and stuck out my stomach—anything to look heavier. Too late. Everyone was already turning to me. Rats. Sometimes being the Light Weight Wimp of the World has its drawbacks.

"It would be perfectly safe," Miguel urged.

"I uh, I don't know, guys . . ." I stalled as I nervously pushed up my glasses.

"Come on, Wally," Opera encouraged.

"You can do it," Wall Street grinned.

"Besides," Miguel threw me another one of his little smiles, "if you really trust God, it shouldn't be a problem, right? . . . Right?"

"But . . . but . . ." I desperately searched my mind for an excuse. Anything would do. Anything at all.

"But what?" Miguel asked.

"But . . . I'm all out of breath mints."

Chapter 8

Uh-oh

It wasn't the most comfortable night I'd ever had. Despite the rumors, hard ground is not good for your back, rocks do not make good pillows, and a giant flattened-out balloon makes a terrible blanket.

But the company was good. After our little talk and prayer, everyone seemed a bit more relaxed. Even Opera was less scared.

"You're starting to get the hang of this, aren't you?" I asked as we all settled in for the night.

"A little," he admitted. "But I'm still not going to sleep."

"Why not?"

"If I'm going to be killed by a bear, I at least want to be awake to remember the details!"

With that, he crawled under the balloon ("for warmth," he said), lay down ("for comfort," he insisted), closed his eyes ("to rest them," he explained), . . . and promptly started to snore.

Good ol' Opera . . .

Wall Street and Miguel were the next to drop off. But not before Wall Street tried to talk more to her brother about God. She didn't get far.

"Look, Sis," he cut her off. "I know what you're trying to do, and I appreciate it. But it's like I told Momma, 'I'm not ready to listen' . . . not yet."

There was kind of a long uneasy tension. Maybe even a couple of sniffles from Wall Street's side of the balloon. But eventually they both dozed off.

It took me a little while longer to get to sleep. Well, if you can call what I did "sleep." Sure, my eyes were closed, but my imagination was going full throttle. And since I'd left ol' Betsy back at the lodge, there was only one place for that imagination to work . . . in my dreams.

Suddenly I was watching Ecology-Man clinging to the boulder for his life as Toxoid Breath tried to suck him into the vacuum cleaner. . . .

Just when our handsome hero is about to lose his grip (in more ways than one), the vacuum cleaner starts sparking and shorting out.

"What's going on?" Toxoid Breath bellows.

Ecology-Man spots one of his beaver friends from the forest gnawing into the electric cord.

"Beave, don't!" Ecology-Man shouts. "You'll be electrocuted!"

But ol' Beave doesn't listen. His brother, Wally, and his parents, Mr. and Mrs. Cleaver, have already been trapped and shipped off to Rerun-land. Now it's just him and Eddie Haskel . . . which is more than the Beave can stand.

Quicker than you can say, "Look out, here come the puns," ol' Beave takes one last bite into the electric cord, and:

- He *lights up* like a Christmas tree.
- Talk about a *shocking* experience.
- I mean the moment is really *electrifying*.
- It is *charged* with *high voltage* action.

Had enough? No? Well here's a few more...

- It is full of *power*.
- In *short*, it's a real *hot* and *current* moment.

In other words . . .

POOF, ZIT, CRACKLE, POP . . . The vacuum cleaner shuts down faster than the school building on Friday afternoon.

Suddenly Molly the Mole pops up underneath our hero. Suddenlier still, she drags him down into her underground tunnel.

"Thanks, Molly," our hero gasps, as he glances around the tunnel. "Hey, I like what you've done with the place. When did you add the tennis courts?"

"Zzee zzame time we builtzz zee zzwimming pool," she says whistling through her big front teeth.

RRRRRRRRRRRRRR . . .

"What'zz zzat?" Molly whistles.

Suddenly a drill bit the size of a Buick crashes through her ceiling.

RRRRRRRRRRRRRR . . .

Then another . . . and another.

"Zzomebody muzzt be drilling for oil!"

"No way," our hero shouts. "It's Toxoid Breath, and he's drilling for me!"

With a quick good-bye kiss on the cheek from Molly, Ecology-Man scurries out of the mole hole to confront the troublesome tyrant.

But Toxoid Breath has only begun to

terrorize. Quickly he produces a dozen cans of orange spray paint. And quicklier still he sprays graffiti on everything he can find . . . rocks, trees, old Ross Perot bumper stickers.

Now it's time for Ecology-Man to call upon his super powers of nature. Now it's time to use what only super-trained superheroes like himself (so don't try this at home, kids) are qualified to use. He throws back his head and cries to the heavens:

> "Oh, heavenly lights be gone from
>   hither,
> Help me make this monster
>   quiver!"

And, just like that, the sun disappears. (A neat trick for 1:30 in the afternoon, but remember this is my story, so I can do anything I want.) Quickly ol' bio-boy draws his slide projector from his slide projector holster and fires off a series of pictures. There's a slide of a rain forest! Then a spotted owl! Then baby seals that *haven't* been clobbered!

"No, stop!" Toxoid Breath screams.
Our hero continues the attack. He
shows streams *without* pollution. Coast-
lines *without* oil spills!
"It's too pure to look at! Stop it!
Stop it!!"
It's time to finish him off. Our hero
twists open a bottle of Mountain Spring
Drinking Water and starts chugging it
down.
"Noooo!!" Toxoid Breath shouts as he
rolls backward. "There's no *toxins*[3] in
that—no *sulfides*[4], no lead deposits,
it's too healthy—STOP!"
Our whole-grain good guy raises the
bottle high over his head. He approaches
the *bio-hazardous*[5] bad guy. "I think it's
time to clean up your act!" He grins.
"No, please . . . " the tearful tyrant
begs as he retreats.
Closer and closer Ecology-Man comes.
"Please, please—keep it away . . .
anything but that!"
And then . . . oh no . . . Toxoid Breath
has one more trick up his corroded

---

3. TOXINS: poisons
4. SULFIDES: a type of pollution
5. BIO-HAZARDOUS: harmful to the environment

sleeve! He produces 100 cans of aerosol hair spray. He begins spraying each
and every one, which releases tons of
fluorocarbons[6] into the air. Soon a
giant hole forms in the *ozone layer*[7].
Suddenly sunbathers on beaches are
getting tans in thirty seconds. They
look like shriveled raisins in forty-
five. And in less than an a minute,
they're reduced to piles of cancerous
ash.

"Give it up, Ecology-Man," he hisses.
"Become my prisoner, or I'll turn the
earth into such a greenhouse, you'll be
growing orchids in your freezer!"

Our organically-grown hero has no
choice. He drops his slide projector and
Mountain Spring Water to the ground. The
vile villain picks him up. Next, Toxoid Breath opens his iron mouth and poisonous fumes rise from his toxic-waste
stomach. Ecology-Man is about to be destroyed.

---

6. FLUOROCARBONS: a type of air pollution
that can come from aerosol spray cans.
7. OZONE LAYER: the part of the earth's atmo-
sphere that protects us from the harmful rays
of the sun but that can be destroyed by
fluorocarbons.

Now there is no one to stop the spread
of worldwide pollution. Now the earth
will be covered in smog and concrete.
Now department stores will change their
elevator music from Barry Manilow to U-2
. . . (well, I guess every cloud has a
silver lining). Still, what will we do?
How will we survive?
And then—

But there was no "then." Unfortunately I woke
up. Even more unfortunately, it was morning. I
would have kept thinking about my story on saving the world but I had a minor distraction to at-
tend to . . .
Like saving myself.

*   *   *   *   *

"Okay . . . Sis, Opera—"
Miguel coughed again. It was hard for him to
talk, but he forced himself. He had to. He was a lot
weaker than last night, and we had to get him to
a hospital . . . soon, real soon.
"Pull open the mouth," he ordered. "Spread it
out good and wide to catch the wind."

Opera and Wall Street obeyed and pulled open the mouth of the deflated balloon. Immediately the breeze started to rush inside, filling it.

"Good thing we landed on this ridge," I shouted to Miguel as I tilted the basket and burner on the ground for him to fire.

He nodded. "Landings and takeoffs are a bear, but at least this wind will fill the balloon."

He was right. The wind quickly shoved air into the balloon. The only thing I'd ever seen fill quicker was Opera's mouth when he had a bag of corn chips.

"Have you got that bungee cord tied to the basket good and tight?" Miguel asked.

I nodded.

He craned his neck for a better look. "Better knot it a couple more times, just to be sure."

He didn't have to ask twice. I'd already tied the other end to a distant tree. Don't get me wrong. I was no Boy Scout. I only knew one type of knot. But I figured with enough loops, tangles, overlapping tangles and more overlapping tangles something was bound to stick.

"Now go down to the top of the balloon and hold that crown line steady like last time." Miguel started coughing again. "It's going to be rough, so hang on!"

He wasn't fooling about the rough part. I ran down, wrapped the rope around my hand, and immediately started getting whipped about. First to the left, then the right. It was like a crazy dance—like the Hokey Pokey. But instead of "putting my left arm in and my left arm out" the balloon was "throwing my whole body in and my whole body out."

Finally it was inflated. I headed back to the basket where Wall Street and Opera were doing all they could to hold it down.

"GET IN!" Miguel shouted.

"BUT, HOW DO I—"

"I'LL TELL YOU EVERYTHING THROUGH THE WALKIE-TALKIE—JUST GET IN AND KEEP FIRING THE BURNER. HURRY!"

Miguel had brought along an extra walkie-talkie. He kept two in the basket and two in the truck. Once again I showed my athletic abilities by leaping into the basket and landing head first.

"WALLY! . . . *WALLY!*"

"Here," I shouted as I popped back up wearing my famous McDoogle-The-Idiot grin. And why not? If I was going to die, I was at least going to be pleasant about it.

"SQUEEZE THE BURNER HANDLE," Miguel shouted. "KEEP THE FLAME GOING. SQUEEZE IT!"

I reached up to the brass handle, squeezed, and . . .
K-WOOOSH . . .
The flame shot up into the balloon. Seconds
later the basket started to scrape forward.
Miguel shouted to Opera and Wall Street.
"HOLD IT AS LONG AS YOU CAN!"
And they did . . . for a whole three seconds. And
then, just like that, the basket scooted down the
road and took off.
Being a great man of courage, I did what any
great man of courage would do. I yelled my lungs
out . . .
"MICKEY! . . ."
But it did no good. Suddenly I was airborne—
racing over the road like an airplane taking off.
The only problem was my "runway" made a sharp
turn to the left. No problem except the wind didn't.
It just kept going straight! Straight into a giant
stand of trees up ahead. That meant only one
thing. One of those trees was about to have a little
operation. One of them was about to receive a per-
manent McDoogle implant.
"KEEP FIRING THE BURNER," Miguel
shouted, "KEEP FIRING THE BURNER!"
K-WOOOOOSH!
I followed orders perfectly. Unfortunately, the
balloon didn't. Instead of going up, it kept racing
ahead. No way could I clear those trees. I was

heading straight for them. And then, just when
one of the branches was about to perform Open
McDoogle Surgery, the bungee cord reached its
end. It started to stretch. As it stretched, it slowed
me down. As I slowed down, I shot up!

"All right, Wally!" Opera and Wall Street
cheered from below. "Way to go, McDoogle!"

The cord continued to stretch and I continued to
rise. Soon I was above the treetops, and sooner
still the ground wind started to fade. The bucking
and bouncing grew less and less. *Well what do you
know,* I thought, *I finally did something right.*

My walkie-talkie hissed and clicked as Miguel's
voice came through. "Nice work, Wally."

"Thanks," I said, grinning.

"Wally, can you hear me . . . WALLY!"

"Oh, sorry," I said, fumbling with the button, "I
guess I have to push this thing down to talk,
right?"

"Right. Now all you have to do is stay put, fire
that burner when I tell you and everything will
be—"

Suddenly the balloon gave a little shudder.

"What was that?" I asked.

"What was what?"

It shuddered again.

"That?" I repeated.

"Don't worry," Miguel replied. "As long as you

have that bungee cord tied good and tight you're perfectly safe."

I looked down at the cord tied to the basket.

Uh-oh.

"Listen, Miguel, about tying that cord . . . if it should happen to like come undone or anything . . ."

The balloon gave another shudder as the overlapping tangles that I called a "knot" kept unwinding.

"Relax," Miguel assured me.

"But I mean, if it should like happen to . . ."

"If that bungee cord breaks," Miguel chuckled, "you'll know before any of us if there really is a God."

I tried to return the laugh, but it's hard to laugh when your heart's stopping . . . when you're watching a bungee cord finish untangling its last tangle and start slipping away . . . when you feel yourself being shot up into orbit at a billion point eight miles a second.

"Wally . . . WALLY . . ."

"It figures," I muttered. "My whole life reduced to a broken bungee cord . . . a broken bungee cord that isn't even broken."

Chapter 9

Tests of Faith

"Wally, Wally can you hear me? Come in, Wally! Come in!"

I reached down to the walkie-talkie. I knew I had to sound calm. I knew I had to sound relaxed. Maybe a little McDoogle humor would help lighten things up. I pressed the key and screamed:

"HEEELLLPPP!!!"

(So much for humor.)

"It's okay, Wally, we can handle it, we can handle it."

"What do you mean, *we*?" I shouted. "I'm the one stuck up here!"

"And I'm the one stuck down here." He gave a couple of bone-rattling coughs. "And if we don't work together, we'll both be stuck for good."

Well, okay, if he wanted to be that way about it . . .

"You look like you're up about 900 or 1,000 feet. How fast are you rising?"

"I'm not rising," I said. "I'm not moving at all."

"Of course you are. Look down at your variometer."

"My *what-o-meter?*"

"The gauge to your right."

I looked down at the three gauges on the inside of the basket.

"Which direction is the little arrow pointing," he asked, "up or down?"

"Up," I answered. "It's on the 300."

"That's too fast, you're climbing too fast."

"No," I argued, "I'm not moving at all, I don't feel a thing."

"You don't go by feelings up there, Wally—you go by those gauges."

"But—"

"Trust them."

"But if I don't feel anything . . ."

"That's what I'm saying. It's just like what you were preaching about faith last night. You don't go by what you feel, you go by what those gauges say. Up there those gauges are your Bible . . . you got to believe them—nothing else."

"And what I see, what I feel? . . ."

" . . . Don't mean a thing. You just trust those gauges like you're supposed to trust God."

"Now who's preaching?" I quipped.

Miguel gave a little laugh. "For the next few hours we better all believe." He coughed a couple of times and continued. "Now, take that parachute line above your head and give it a little tug. We're going to let out some air and get you to drift back over here."

I gave the rope a tug. The balloon bumped slightly but nothing else seemed to happen. I tried again, holding it down longer this time. Still nothing.

"It's not working."

"Look at your variometer," he said, "what does it read?"

I glanced down at the gauge. "It's starting to point down, but that can't be right. Nothing's happened, I don't feel—"

"Don't trust your feelings, Wally. Trust those gauges."

"Okay," I sighed, "but it doesn't seem right."

"Don't worry, you're doing fine . . . just fine."

"This is obviously a new definition of *fine*," I cracked.

"Just hang on, man . . . you can do this."

And he was right. Slowly, as I trusted the gauges instead of my feelings, we began to make progress. Not all at once, mind you. After all we're still dealing with Wally McDoogle, Dork-oid

Extraordinaire (that's French for *extraordinary*).
But gradually things started to click. Gradually,
Miguel was able to guide me in and out of the right
air currents (by firing the burner or letting out the
air) until I was able to stay in his general area . . .
give or take a few miles.

"Any sign of a plane yet?" Miguel asked. Several
more minutes had passed, and he was sounding a
lot weaker.

I looked around. According to the altimeter I was
about 800 feet up. It was like I could see forever.
Unfortunately, "forever" didn't include any planes.

"Listen," Miguel gave a couple more coughs, "I'm
going to have to turn you over to Sis. I need (more
coughing), I need to take a break."

"You going to be all right?" I asked in concern.

"Don't worry about me." He coughed again. "Just
keep an eye on those instruments."

"Gotcha."

"Hey, Wally." It was Wall Street. For someone
who should be bummed, she sounded pretty good.
"What's happening?"

"Not much," I answered, "just another typical
day in the life of Wally McDoogle."

"You're doing great . . ." she said. "We're all really
proud of you."

I gave a shrug, thankful that walkie-talkies
don't show blushing.

"How's Opera?" I asked.

"He's out in the woods getting more firewood."

"By himself!" I practically shouted. "Isn't he afraid of being attacked by a crazed chipmunk or a herd of slugs or somethin'?"

She giggled. "I guess your faith is kinda contagious, Wally."

More blushing. I tried to change the subject. "How's your brother?" I asked. "He's sounding a lot worse."

"He is," she agreed. Her voice had a little quiver to it, but it also had a little strength. "Me and Opera, we're praying for him, Wally . . . we're praying real hard."

I nodded and said nothing . . . except a quite prayer of my own.

Things had really turned around. Here I was, super chicken of heights, up in the air flying on my own! There was Opera, super chicken of the woods, actually in them by himself. And Wall Street was back to praying again. I tell you, if God was making a point about trusting Him, He wasn't doing a half bad job. Now if He could just do something about—

Then, I heard it. Ever so faintly. "What's that?" I asked.

"What's what?" Wall Street asked back over the walkie-talkie.

I scanned the sky, giving it a quick 360. At first I saw nothing. And then I spotted it. "A plane!" I shouted. "A plane, and it's coming this way!"

"Stay put." It was Miguel's voice again. Weaker than ever. "They've probably seen the balloon, they're coming to investigate."

"Great!" I cried. "All I have to do is float over you guys and they'll see where—"

"Don't do a thing!" Miguel coughed. "Just stay where you are; they'll find us."

"Yeah, but—"

"Stay there, Wally. You've come this far, don't blow it now."

I gave a heavy sigh . . . careful to leave my finger down on the key so he could hear it.

The plane continued to drone toward me. Closer and closer it came. I was getting a little nervous. The thing had two very sharp looking propellers, and I wasn't crazy about either one of 'em. I hadn't worked this hard to be chopped up in some Plane-o-matic.

Finally the plane dipped its wing and circled around me. It was about time. The best I could make out there were four people inside.

I waved.

They waved.

I pointed toward the road.

They pointed toward the road.

I pointed some more.

They pointed some more.

"Come on guys, this isn't 'Simon Says!'" I shouted as I kept jabbing my finger toward the road.

Finally, somebody in the cockpit figured it out. (Rocket scientists, these guys weren't.) The plane veered to the left, and headed in the direction I pointed.

We all waited.

A few seconds later they swooped down and made a tight little turn.

"They found us!" Wall Street shouted through the radio. "They found us!" I could hear them clapping and yelling.

"We did it!" I shouted back. "We did it!"

"Not quite." It was Miguel.

"What do you mean?"

"We still have to get you down."

Oh, that.

"How much fuel you got?"

I looked at the gauge of the last propane tank. "It's almost empty, what do I do?"

"Uh-oh."

"'Uh-oh?'" I said. "What type of order is 'uh-oh?'"

Miguel coughed again. "Look, Wally, you're going to have to find a place, anyplace, and set her down . . . now."

"But—?"

"*Now,* Wally! Drop her now so you have fuel to break your fall!"

'*Drop?*' '*Break?*' '*Fall?*' I didn't like the sound of this one bit!

"Maybe I can get back to your road," I said as I reached up and fired the burner. "Maybe I can—"

"Save your fuel, Wally!"

"But—"

"Save it!"

I released the lever.

"Now pull down your parachute cord. Start letting air out."

I did and shouted, "Where am I going?"

"Look for a break in the trees—any opening at all."

The balloon started to rotate. "Mickey, I'm spinning!

"Let up on the cord—you're falling too fast! Fire the burner!"

I let go of the cord and fired the burner. After a second or two, it started to sputter. Then suddenly the roar stopped. So did the flame . . .

So did my heart.

"MICKEY!"

"Throw out the fuel tanks! Dump any extra weight you can find!"

I quickly unstrapped the fuel tanks and started throwing them over the side. "Bombs away . . . ."

It helped, but not enough. The variometer said I was still heading down, and heading down too fast. "Now what?" I shouted.

No answer.

"Mickey . . . !"

"Crouch down in the basket—protect your head!"

"*What?*"

"You're going to crash, Wally. With any luck you'll hit the trees and they'll break your fall!"

"*HIT* THE TREES!? THAT'S WHAT WE'VE BEEN TRYING TO AVOID!"

"DO IT, WALLY! TRUST ME AND DO IT!"

I took one last look over the edge. Well, if he wanted trees, I had trees. Millions of 'em. And by the way they were racing at me, I knew we were about to become close friends . . . too close.

I crouched down.

"Help him God . . . keep him safe. . . ."

I checked my mouth, but I wasn't saying the words. It came from the radio. It was Miguel. Praying! For me! Granted, it wasn't the world's greatest prayer, but I figured I needed all the help I could get. I managed to squeak out a feeble, "Amen." And just in time.

SCRAPE . . . SCRATCH . . . CRUNCH . . .
I was thrown across the basket.
"Wally, can you hear me?!"
CRUNCH . . . SCRATCH . . . SCRAPE . . .
I was thrown to the other side.
"WALLY!"
CRUNCH . . . SNAP . . . SPLINTER . . .
Back and forth I went. It was like a giant ping-pong match, with me as the ball!

And then, just as suddenly as it started, it stopped. Completely. Nothing, but dead silence.

Speaking of "dead," I had to admit I was a little disappointed. As far as I could tell, heaven looked just like earth. No golden streets, no choir, no hot harp band . . . just me . . . and these trees . . . and—

"Wally . . ." It was the walkie-talkie. "Wally, can you hear me?"

"Great," I muttered, "all that hard work, and I'm still alive."

I got to my knees and worked up enough courage to peer over the edge. In appreciation for my heroics, the basket gave a tip forward, and we fell another fifteen feet.

"AUGHHHHHHH . . ."

Still no ground. After a few more screams and lots more prayers (I figured it didn't hurt to stock up on 'em), I worked up the courage to look over the edge again. The basket was still thirty feet from the ground. Only this time it wasn't doing any more falling. This time the trees had us in a tight, death grip . . . better make that a "life grip." We didn't move. Not an inch. Well, except for the mild swaying of the basket as it rocked back and forth in the breeze.

Boy, do I know how to have a vacation or what? Now if I just had a Diet Coke and a TV remote . . . Of course, a TV to go with the remote wouldn't be bad . . . and a hotel to go with the TV. But, hey, at least I had my life . . .

Good ol' God. He did it again.

Chapter 10

Wrapping Up

I'm not going to bore you with all details on how we got back. You know, things like . . .

—The rescue helicopter picking up Miguel and flying him to the nearest hospital.

—Or the search-and-rescue truck racing down the logging road to get Wall Street and Opera.

—I won't even mention how they had to bring a fire engine all the way out, and use their ladder to pull me from the tree, or how the local TV crew tagged along and got it all on tape.

—And I especially won't bring up the part where my pants got caught on a branch, and the rescuers kept pulling, and the pants kept holding, and the rescuers kept pulling, and the pants kept holding, and the rescuers kept pulling, and . . .

RRRRRRIIIIIIIP . . .

the pants stopped holding. I was free! No
more worries. No more pants for that matter.
Which wasn't too bad, except for the part of
seeing me and my Fruit of the Looms on the
six o'clock news.

I won't bore you with any of that stuff. Instead,
I'll tell you about our last meeting with Miguel. He
was in the hospital all stretched out like a human
trampoline.

The guy was right about his body. Lots of stuff
was broken. But the doctors said in time he'd be as
good as new. Still, his mom wanted to stay with
him a few more days (or months), just in case. (You
know how moms are.)

So she had us all packed and ready to go home
by bus. Dad would pick us up when we got there.
On the way to the station, we swung by Miguel's
hospital room to say good-bye.

"Sorry about your vacation," he said, as we
entered.

"Hey, it was great!" Opera shouted over his
Walkman. "Everything was super . . . being out in
the wild, living off the land, being one with nature.
Think we can do it again next year?"

We all gave him a look.

He shrugged and flipped his tape over.

"Sorry about your balloon," I offered.

"Don't sweat it," Miguel grinned. "You did a great job!"

"Yeah . . . I guess I kinda did, didn't I?"

"Like a pro."

"Of course, I had a little help," I said throwing a look up to heaven.

Miguel frowned. "You're not going to start preaching again are you, McDoogle?"

"No . . . well, yeah, maybe a little." I smiled. "What about you—you going to start listening?"

He shot back a smile of his own, "No . . . well, yeah, maybe a little."

We held each other's smile until Wall Street stepped in. "God really did help us out, didn't He? I mean, everything we prayed for, He answered."

"I suppose," Miguel said, trying to adjust himself. "Though I could have done without the extra bruises and broken bones."

"Might be His way of getting your attention," his mom suggested.

Miguel gave her a look. "Now, how did I know you were going to say something like that?"

"Oh, I'll be saying a lot more than that." She smiled. "Now that I have a captive audience, I'll be saying a whole lot more."

Miguel pretended to groan as we all laughed and moved in to say final good-byes.

Wall Street was right. God really did come through for us. . . .

—Opera was no longer petrified of the great outdoors.

—Wall Street's prayers about her brother were finally starting to be answered.

—And me? Who knows, maybe I'll finally be able to start riding escalators with my eyes open.

A few minutes later we were at the bus station saying good-byes to Wall Street's mom. Of course, the two of them cried and did the usual mom and daughter stuff.

Once that was over, we climbed on board, and I did my famous "McDoogle Trip-And-Fall-On-My-Face" routine (the one I've been perfecting for years). With lots of good-bye waves and a couple more tears from Wall Street, the bus pulled away and we finally settled in for the long ride home.

After the first hundred or so times of reliving our adventure (with each of us being our own hero), things got a little boring. I whipped out ol' Betsy and turned her on. It was time to finish Ecology-Man's turbulent and troublesome tussle with the tyrannically terrible (try tumbling those t's over your tired tongue without tripping) . . . Toxoid Breath!

When we last left our no-preservatives-added good guy, he was about to be eaten by Toxoid Breath. Seems he made a little deal. Ecology-Man would let this bad boy destroy him in exchange for . . . er, uh . . . for getting to be destroyed. (Our hero was never too good at business deals.)

But suddenly Molly the Mole reappears from her hole. Behind her she drags a bag of her recyclable pop cans.

The sight startles Toxoid Breath—but for only a second. He has a dinner date with our hero that he doesn't want to miss.

Taking his cue from Molly, ol' Griz the bear races to his den and pulls out all the recyclable plastics from his garbage.

"What are you doing?" Toxoid Breath shouts. "Stop it, stop it at once!"

Soon the other woodland creatures catch on. Soon everyone begins to recycle . . .

putting their paper in one pile, plastic
in another, aluminum in another.
   The sight is too much. Toxoid Breath
starts to quiver. Then tremble. Then
shake, rattle, and roll.
   And still the animals continue...

   — The woodchucks agree to cut
     back watering their lawns.
   — The coyotes shorten their showers.

It's too much for the horrible hunk of
junk. He drops Ecology-Man and screams
. . . "STOP IT . . . YOU'RE DESTROYING
ME!"
   But the animals continue:

   — The gophers agree to use low-
     wattage light bulbs.
   — The toads agree to convert to
     solar power.

   Toxoid Breath's bolts begin to pop
loose. His seams begin to split. And
still the animals continue their attack.
   — Owls start recycling newspapers.
   — Rainbow trout start carpooling.

And then it happens. All this concern for the environment is more than Toxoid Breath can handle. He blows his stack . . . literally.

KA-BOOOOOOM!!!!

Smoke and metal fly everywhere. The woodland creatures cheer.

But their celebration is short-lived. In the midst of the smoke and debris, there is a stirring. Everyone holds their breath. Is he coming back to life? Is there no way to destroy this mechanical menace?

Then out from the smoking wreckage stumbles . . . Kirby the vacuum cleaner salesman. "Hi, there. Boy look at this place. What a mess. But no job is too big for Kirby." Now that he's free, he can again use his machine for good. He flips on the vacuum cleaner and starts cleaning up.

The forest creatures cheer as they race to our hero and lift him to their shoulders. Together they have saved the planet. Together they have made the world a cleaner, safer (if not more fanatical) place to live.

But that is not the end, dear reader. Who knows who our superhero will be next time? Who knows what fearsome foe he will fight? So hang onto your hats (especially if Kirby keeps running that vacuum cleaner of his). There's no telling what's in store....